SCIENTISTS V
AT AN ASTO...

Then Tom Betterton, a brilliant nuclear physicist, vanished. But Scotland Yard, the F.B.I. and the Secret Services of other countries still could not discover the pattern.

Betterton's wife possibly knew more than she was telling, but except for a last strange warning, she couldn't tell any more—she'd died after a plane crash in Casablanca.

So another woman agreed to impersonate the dead woman. As Mrs. Thomas Betterton she could lead government agents to her missing "husband." The improbable masquerade led her deeper and deeper into the African wastelands and closer and closer to the center of the plot— and to death!

SO MANY STEPS TO DEATH
was originally published by
Dodd, Mead & Company, Inc.

Books by Agatha Christie

The A.B.C. Murders
At Bertram's Hotel
The Body in the Library
By the Pricking of My Thumbs
A Caribbean Mystery
Cat Among the Pigeons
The Clocks
Crooked House
Dead Man's Folly
Death Comes as the End
Easy to Kill (Original British title: Murder Is Easy)
Endless Night
Evil Under the Sun
Funerals Are Fatal
Hallowe'en Party
Hickory Dickory Death (Original British title: Hickory, Dickory, Dock)
The Mirror Crack'd (Original British title: The Mirror Crack'd from Side to Side)
Mrs. McGinty's Dead
A Murder Is Announced
The Murder of Roger Ackroyd

Murder On The Orient Express (Also published as Murder In The Calais Coach)
Murder with Mirrors (Original British title: They Do It with Mirrors)
The Mystery of the Blue Train
Nemesis
Ordeal by Innocence
The Pale Horse
Passenger to Frankfurt
Peril at End House
A Pocket Full of Rye
Remembered Death (Original British title: Sparkling Cyanide)
So Many Steps to Death (Original British title: Destination Unknown)
Ten Little Indians (Also published as And Then There Were None)
Third Girl
Towards Zero
What Mrs. McGillicuddy Saw (Original British title: 4:50 from Paddington)

Published by POCKET BOOKS

AGATHA CHRISTIE

So Many Steps to Death

(Original British title: Destination Unknown)

PUBLISHED BY POCKET BOOKS NEW YORK

SO MANY STEPS TO DEATH

Dodd, Mead edition published 1955

POCKET BOOK edition published June, 1956
7th printing .... December, 1975

L

This POCKET BOOK edition includes every word contained in the original, higher-priced edition. It is printed from brand-new plates made from completely reset, clear, easy-to-read type. POCKET BOOK editions are published by POCKET BOOKS, a division of Simon & Schuster, Inc., 630 Fifth Avenue, New York, N.Y. 10020. Trademarks registered in the United States and other countries.

**TO
ANTHONY**

*who likes foreign travel
as much as I do*

Cast of Characters

So Many
Steps
to Death

1

THE MAN BEHIND THE DESK moved a heavy glass paper weight four inches to the right. His face was not so much thoughtful or abstracted as expressionless. He had the pale complexion that comes from living most of the day in artificial light. This man, you felt, was an indoor man. A man of desks and files. The fact that to reach his office you had to walk through long twisting underground corridors was somehow strangely appropriate. It would have been difficult to guess his age. He looked neither old nor young. His face was smooth and unwrinkled, and in his eyes was a great tiredness.

The other man in the room was older. He was dark with a small military moustache. There was about him an alert nervous energy. Even now, unable to sit still, he was pacing up and down, from time to time throwing off a remark in a jerky manner.

"Reports!" he said explosively. "Reports, reports and more reports, and none of them any damn good!"

The man at the desk looked down at the papers in front of him. On top was an official card headed, "Betterton, Thomas Charles." After the name was an interrogation mark. The man at the desk nodded thoughtfully. He said,

"You've followed up these reports and none of them any good?"

The other shrugged his shoulders.

"How can one tell?" he asked.

The man behind the desk sighed.

11

"Yes," he said, "there is that. One can't tell really."

The older man went on with a kind of machine gun volley abruptness,

"Reports from Rome; reports from Touraine; seen on the Riviera; noticed in Antwerp; definitely identified in Oslo; positively seen in Biarritz; observed behaving suspiciously in Strasbourg; seen on the beach at Ostend with a glamorous blonde; noticed walking in the streets in Brussels with a greyhound! Hasn't been seen yet in the Zoo with his arm round a zebra, but I daresay that will come!"

"You've no particular fancy yourself, Wharton? Personally I had hopes of the Antwerp report, but it hasn't led to anything. Of course by now . . ." the young man stopped speaking and seemed to go into a coma. Presently he came out of it again and said cryptically, "Yes, probably . . . and yet—I wonder?"

Colonel Wharton sat down abruptly on the arm of a chair.

"But we've got to find out," he said insistently. "We've got to break the back of all this *how* and *why* and *where?* You can't lose a tame scientist every month or so and have no idea *how* they go or *why* they go or *where!* Is it where we think—or isn't it? We've always taken it for granted that it is, but now I'm not so sure. You've read all the last dope on Betterton from America?"

The man behind the desk nodded.

"Usual Left Wing tendencies at the period when everyone had them. Nothing of a lasting or permanent nature as far as can be found out. Did sound work before the war though nothing spectacular. When Mannheim escaped from Germany Betterton was assigned as Assistant to him, and ended by marrying Mannheim's daughter. After Mannheim's death he carried on, on his own, and did brilliant work. He leaped into fame with the startling discovery of ZE Fission. ZE Fission was a brilliant and absolutely revolutionary discovery. It put Betterton absolutely tops. He was all set for a brilliant career over there, but his wife had died soon after their marriage and he was all broken up over it. He came to England. He has been at Harwell for the last eighteen months. Just six months ago he married again."

"Anything there?" asked Wharton sharply.

The other shook his head.

"Not that we can find out. She's the daughter of a local solicitor. Worked in an insurance office before her marriage. No violent political affinities so far as we've been able to discover."

"ZE Fission," said Colonel Wharton gloomily, with distaste. "What they mean by all these terms beats me. I'm old fashioned. I never really even visualised a molecule, but here they are nowadays splitting up the universe! Atom bombs, Nuclear fission, ZE fission, and all the rest of it. And Betterton was one of the splitters in chief! What do they say of him at Harwell?"

"Quite a pleasant personality. As to his work, nothing outstanding or spectacular. Just variations on the practical applications of ZE."

Both men were silent for a moment. Their conversation had been desultory, almost automatic. The security reports lay in a pile on the desk and the security reports had had nothing of value to tell.

"He was thoroughly screened on arrival here, of course," said Wharton.

"Yes, everything was quite satisfactory."

"Eighteen months ago," said Wharton thoughtfully. "It gets 'em down, you know. Security precautions. The feeling of being perpetually under the microscope, the cloistered life. They get nervy, queer. I've seen it often enough. They begin to dream of an ideal world. Freedom and brotherhood, and pool-all-secrets and work for the good of humanity! That's exactly the moment when someone who's more or less the dregs of humanity, sees his chance and takes it!" He rubbed his nose. "Nobody's so gullible as the scientist," he said. "All the phony mediums say so. Can't quite see why."

The other smiled, a very tired smile.

"Oh, yes," he said, "it would be so. They think they *know*, you see. That's always dangerous. Now, our kind are different. We're humble minded men. We don't expect to save the world, only pick up one or two broken pieces and remove a monkey wrench or two when it's jamming up the works." He tapped thoughtfully on the table with his finger. "If I only knew a little more about Betterton," he said. "Not his life and actions, but the revealing, everyday things. What sort of jokes he laughed at. What made him swear. Who were the people he admired and who made him mad."

Wharton looked at him curiously.

"What about the wife—you've tried her?"

"Several times."

"Can't she help?"

The other shrugged his shoulders.

"She hasn't so far."

"You think she knows something?"

"She doesn't admit, of course, that she knows anything. All the established reactions: worry, grief, desperate anxiety, no cue or suspicion beforehand, husband's life perfectly normal, no stress of any kind—and so on and so on. Her own theory is that he's been kidnapped."

"And you don't believe her?"

"I'm handicapped," said the man behind the desk bitterly. "I never believe anybody."

"Well," said Wharton slowly, "I suppose one has to keep an open mind. What's she like?"

"Ordinary sort of woman you'd meet any day playing bridge."

Wharton nodded comprehendingly.

"That makes it more difficult," he said.

"She's here to see me now. We shall go over all the same ground again."

"It's the only way," said Wharton. *"I* couldn't do it, though. Haven't got the patience." He got up. "Well, I won't keep you. We've not got much further, have we?"

"Unfortunately, no. You might do a special check up on that Oslo report. It's a likely spot."

Wharton nodded and went out. The other man raised the receiver by his elbow and said:

"I'll see Mrs. Betterton now. Send her in."

He sat staring into space until there was a tap on the door and Mrs. Betterton was shown in. She was a tall woman, about twenty-seven years of age. The most noticeable thing about her was a most magnificent head of auburn red hair. Beneath the splendour of this, her face seemed almost insignificant. She had the blue eyes and light eyelashes that so often go with red hair. She was wearing no make-up, he noticed. He considered the significance of that while he was greeting her, settling her comfortably in a chair near the desk. It inclined him very slightly to the belief that Mrs. Betterton knew more than she had said she knew.

In his experience, women suffering from violent grief and anxiety did not neglect their make-up. Aware of the ravages grief made in their appearance, they did their best to repair those ravages. He wondered if Mrs. Betterton calculatingly abstained from make-up, the better to sustain the part of the distracted wife. She said now, rather breathlessly,

"Oh, Mr. Jessop, I do hope——is there any news?"

He shook his head and said gently,

"I'm so sorry to ask you to come up like this, Mrs.

Betterton. I'm afraid we haven't got any definite news for you."

Olive Betterton said quickly,

"I know. You said so in your letter. But I wondered if—since then—oh! I was glad to come up. Just sitting at home wondering and brooding—that's the worst of it all. Because there's nothing one *can* do!"

The man called Jessop said soothingly:

"You mustn't mind, Mrs. Betterton, if I go over the same ground again and again, ask you the same questions, stress the same points. You see it's always possible that some small point *might* arise. Something that you hadn't thought of before, or perhaps hadn't thought worth mentioning."

"Yes. Yes, I understand. Ask me all over again about everything."

"The last time you saw your husband was on the 23rd of August?"

"Yes."

"That was when he left England to go to Paris to a Conference there."

"Yes."

Jessop went on rapidly,

"He attended the first two days of the Conference. The third day he did not turn up. Apparently he had mentioned to one of his colleagues that he was going instead for a trip on a *bateau mouche* that day."

"A *bateau mouche?* What's a *bateau mouche?*"

Jessop smiled.

"One of those small boats that go along the Seine." He looked at her sharply. "Does that strike you as unlike your husband?"

She said doubtfully,

"It does, rather. I should have thought he'd be so keen on what was going on at the Conference."

"Possibly. Still the subject for discussion on this particular day was not one in which he had any special interest, so he might reasonably have given himself a day off. But it doesn't strike you as being quite like your husband?"

She shook her head.

"He did not return that evening to his hotel," went on Jessop. "As far as can be ascertained he did not pass any frontier, certainly not on his own passport. Do you think he could have had a second passport, in another name perhaps?"

"Oh, no, why should he?"

He watched her.

"You never saw such a thing in his possession?"

She shook her head with vehemence.

"No, and I don't believe it. I don't believe it for a moment. I don't believe he went away deliberately as you all try to make out. Something's happened to him, or else—or else perhaps he's lost his memory."

"His health had been quite normal?"

"Yes. He was working rather hard and sometimes felt a little tired, nothing more than that."

"He'd not seemed worried in any way or depressed?"

"He wasn't worried or depressed about *anything!*" With shaking fingers she opened her bag and took out her handkerchief. "It's all so awful." Her voice shook. "I can't believe it. He'd never have gone off without a word to me. Something's happened to him. He's been kidnapped or he's been attacked perhaps. I try not to think it but sometimes I feel that that must be the solution. He must be dead."

"Now please, Mrs. Betterton, please—there's no need to entertain that supposition yet. If he's dead, his body would have been discovered by now."

"It might not. Awful things happen. He might have been drowned or pushed down a sewer. I'm sure anything could happen in Paris."

"Paris, I can assure you, Mrs. Betterton, is a very well policed city."

She took the handkerchief away from her eyes and stared at him with sharp anger.

"I know what you think, but it isn't so! Tom wouldn't sell secrets or betray secrets. He wasn't a communist. His whole life is an open book."

"What were his political beliefs, Mrs. Betterton?"

"In America he was a Democrat, I believe. Here he voted Labour. He wasn't interested in politics. He was a scientist, first and last." She added defiantly, "He was a brilliant scientist."

"Yes," said Jessop, "he was a brilliant scientist. That's really the crux of the whole matter. He might have been offered, you know, very considerable inducements to leave this country and go elsewhere."

"It's not true." Anger leapt out again. "That's what the papers try to make out. That's what you all think when you come questioning me. It's not true. He'd never go without telling me, without giving me some idea."

"And he told you—nothing?"

Again he was watching her keenly.

"Nothing. I don't know where he is. I think he was kidnapped, or else, as I say, dead. But if he's dead, I must know. I must know soon. I can't go on like this, waiting and wondering. I can't eat or sleep. I'm sick and ill with worry. Can't you help me? Can't you help me *at all?*"

He got up then and moved round his desk. He murmured,

"I'm so very sorry, Mrs. Betterton, so very sorry. Let me assure you that we are trying our very best to find out what has happened to your husband. We get reports in every day from various places."

"Reports from where?" she asked sharply. "What do they say?"

He shook his head.

"They all have to be followed up, sifted and tested. But as a rule, I am afraid, they're vague in the extreme."

"I must *know*," she murmured brokenly again. "I can't go on like this."

"Do you care for your husband very much, Mrs. Betterton?"

"Of course I care for him. Why, we've only been married six months. Only six months."

"Yes, I know. There was—forgive me for asking—no quarrel of any kind between you?"

"Oh, *no!*"

"No trouble over any other woman?"

"Of course not. I've told you. We were only married last April."

"Please believe that I'm not suggesting such a thing is likely, but one has to take every possibility into account that might allow for his going off in this way. You say he had not been upset lately, or worried—not on edge—not nervy in any way?"

"No, no, *no!*"

"People do get nervy, you know, Mrs. Betterton, in such a job as your husband had. Living under exacting security conditions. In fact—" he smiled, "—it's almost normal to be nervy."

She did not smile back.

"He was just as usual," he said stolidly.

"Happy about his work? Did he discuss it at all with you?"

"No, it was all so technical."

"You don't think he had any qualms over its—destructive possibilities, shall I say? Scientists do feel that sometimes."

"He never said anything of the kind."

"You see, Mrs. Betterton," he leaned forward over the desk, dropping some of his impassiveness, "what I am trying to do is to get a picture of your husband. The sort of man he was. And somehow you're not helping me."

"But what more can I say or do? I've answered all your questions."

"Yes, you've answered my questions, mostly in the negative. I want something positive, something constructive. Do you see what I mean? You can look for a man so much better when you know what kind of a man he is."

She reflected for a moment. "I see. At least, I suppose I see. Well, Tom was cheerful and good-tempered. And clever, of course."

Jessop smiled.

"That's a list of qualities. Let's try and get more personal. Did he read much?"

"Yes, a fair amount."

"What sort of books?"

"Oh, biographies. Pook Society recommendations, crime stories if he was tired."

"Rather a conventional reader, in fact. No special preferences? Did he play cards or chess?"

"He played bridge. We used to play with Dr. Evans and his wife once or twice a week."

"Did your husband have many friends?"

"Oh, yes, he was a good mixer."

"I didn't mean just that. I mean was he a man who —cared very much for his friends?"

"He played golf with one or two of our neighbours."

"No special friends or cronies of his own?"

"No. You see, he'd been in the U.S.A. for so long, and he was born in Canada. He didn't know many people over here."

Jessop consulted a scrap of paper at his elbow.

"Three people visited him recently from the States, I understand. I have their names here. As far as we can discover, these three were the only people with whom he recently made contact from *outside*, so to speak. That's why we've given them special attention. Now first, Walter Griffiths. He came to see you at Harwell."

"Yes, he was over in England on a visit and he came to look up Tom."

"And your husband's reactions?"

"Tom was surprised to see him, but very pleased. They'd known each other quite well in the States."

"What did this Griffiths seem like to you? Just describe him in your own way."

"But surely you know all about him?"

"Yes, we know all about him. But I want to hear what you thought of him."

She reflected for a moment.

"Well, he was solemn and rather long-winded. Very polite to me and seemed very fond of Tom and anxious to tell him about things that had happened after Tom had come to England. All local gossip I suppose. It wasn't very interesting to me because I didn't know any of the people. Anyway, I was getting dinner ready while they were reminiscing."

"No question of politics came up?"

"You're trying to hint that he was a communist," Olive Betterton's face flushed. "I'm sure he was nothing of the sort. He had some government job—in the District Attorney's office, I think. And anyway when Tom said something laughing about witch hunts in America, he said solemnly that we didn't understand over here. They were *necessary*. So that shows he *wasn't* a communist!"

"Please, please, Mrs. Betterton, now don't get upset."

"Tom wasn't a communist! I keep telling you so and you don't believe me."

"Yes, I do, but the point is bound to come up. Now for the second contact from abroad, Dr. Mark Lucas. You ran across him in London in the Dorset."

"Yes. We'd gone up to do a show and we were having supper at the Dorset afterwards. Suddenly this man, Luke or Lucas, came along and greeted Tom. He was a research chemist of some kind and the last time he had seen Tom was in the States. He was a German refugee who'd taken American nationality. But surely you . . ."

"But surely I know that? Yes, I do, Mrs. Betterton. Was your husband surprised to see him?"

"Yes, very surprised."

"Pleased?"

"Yes, yes—I think so—"

"But you're not sure?" He pressed her.

"Well, he was a man Tom didn't much care about, or so he told me afterwards, that's all."

"It was just a casual meeting? There was no arrangement made to meet at some future date?"

"No, it was just a casual encounter."

"I see. The third contact from abroad was a woman, Mrs. Carol Speeder, also from the States. How did that come about?"

"She was something to do with UNO, I believe. She'd known Tom in America, and she rang him up from London to say she was over here, and asked if we could come up and lunch one day."

"And did you?"

"No."

"*You* didn't, but your husband did!"

"What!" She stared.

"He didn't tell you?"

"No."

Olive Betterton looked bewildered and uneasy. The

man questioning her felt a little sorry for her, but he did not relent. For the first time he thought he might be getting somewhere.

"I don't understand it," she said uncertainly. "It seems very odd he shouldn't have said anything about it to me."

"They lunched together at the Dorset where Mrs. Speeder was staying, on Wednesday August 12th."

"August 12th?"

"Yes."

"Yes, he did go to London about then. . . . He never said anything—" she broke off again, and then shot out a question. "What is she like?"

He answered quickly and reassuringly.

"Not at all a glamorous type, Mrs. Betterton. A competent young career woman of thirty-odd, not particularly good-looking. There's absolutely no suggestion of her ever having been on intimate terms with your husband. That is just why it's odd that he didn't tell you about the meeting."

"Yes, yes, I see that."

"Now think carefully, Mrs. Betterton. Did you notice any change in your husband about that time? About the middle of August, shall we say? That would be about a week before the conference."

"No—No, I noticed nothing. There was nothing to notice."

Jessop sighed.

The instrument on his desk buzzed discreetly. He picked up the receiver.

"Yes," he said.

The voice at the other end said,

"There's a man who's asking to see someone in authority about the Betterton case, sir."

"What's his name?"

The voice at the other end coughed discreetly.

"Well, I'm not exactly sure how you pronounce it, Mr. Jessop. Perhaps I'd better spell it."

"Right. Go ahead."

He jotted down on his blotter the letters as they came over the wire.

"Polish?" he said interrogatively, at the end.

"He didn't say, sir. He speaks English quite well, but with a bit of an accent."

"Ask him to wait."

"Very good, sir."

Jessop replaced the telephone. Then he looked across at Olive Betterton. She sat there quite quietly with a disarming, hopeless placidity. He tore off the leaf on his desk pad with the name he had just written on it, and shoved it across to her.

"Know anybody of that name?" he asked.

Her eyes widened as she looked at it. For a moment he thought she looked frightened.

"Yes," she said. "Yes, I do. He wrote to me."

"When?"

"Yesterday. He's a cousin of Tom's first wife. He's just arrived in this country. He was very concerned about Tom's disappearance. He wrote to ask if I had had any news and—and to give me his most profound sympathy."

"You'd never heard of him before that?"

She shook her head.

"Ever hear your husband speak of him?"

"No."

"So really he mightn't be your husband's cousin at all?"

"Well, no, I suppose not. I never thought of that." She looked startled. "But Tom's first wife was a foreigner. She was Professor Mannheim's daughter. This man seemed to know all about her and Tom in his letter. It was very correct and formal and—and foreign, you know. It seemed quite genuine. And anyway, what would be the point—if he weren't genuine, I mean?"

"Ah, that's what one always asks oneself." Jessop smiled faintly. "We do it so much here that we begin to see the smallest thing quite out of proportion!"

"Yes, I should think you might." She shivered suddenly. "It's like this room of yours, in the middle of a labyrinth of corridors, just like a dream when you think you will never get out. . . ."

"Yes, yes, I can see it might have a claustrophobic effect," said Jessop pleasantly.

Olive Betterton put a hand up and pushed back her hair from her forehead.

"I can't stand it much longer, you know," she said. "Just sitting and waiting. I want to get away somewhere for a change. Abroad for choice. Somewhere where reporters won't ring me up all the time, and people stare at me. I'm always meeting friends and they keep asking if I have had any news." She paused, then went on, "I think—I think I'm going to break down. I've tried to be brave, but it's too much for me. My doctor agrees. He says I ought to go right away somewhere for three or four weeks. He wrote me a letter. I'll show you."

She fumbled in her bag, took out an envelope and pushed it across the desk to Jessop.

"You'll see what he says."

Jessop took the letter out of the envelope and read it.

"Yes," he said. "Yes, I see."

He put the letter back in the envelope.

"So—so it would be all right for me to go?" Her eyes watched him nervously.

"But of course, Mrs. Betterton," he replied. He raised surprised eyebrows. "Why not?"

"I thought you might object."

"Object—why? It's entirely your own business. You'll arrange it so that I can get in touch with you while you're away in case any news should come through."

"Oh, of course."

"Where were you thinking of going?"

"Somewhere where there is sun and not too many English people. Spain or Morocco."

"Very nice. Do you a lot of good, I'm sure."

"Oh, thank you. Thank you very much."

She rose, excited, elated—her nervousness still apparent.

Jessop rose, shook hands with her, pressed the buzzer for a messenger to see her out. He went back to his chair and sat down. For a few moments his face remained as expressionless as before, then very slowly he smiled. He lifted the phone.

"I'll see Major Glydr now," he said.

2

"MAJOR GLYDR?" Jessop hesitated a little over the name.

"It is difficult, yes." The visitor spoke with humorous appreciation. "Your compatriots, they have called me Glider in the war. And now, in the States, I shall change my name to Glyn, which is more convenient for all."

"You come from the States now?"

"Yes, I arrive a week ago. You are—excuse me—Mr. Jessop?"

"I'm Jessop."

The other looked at him with interest.

"So," he said. "I have heard of you."

"Indeed? From whom?"

The other smiled.

"Perhaps we go too fast. Before you permit that I should ask you some questions, I present you first this letter from the U.S. Embassy."

He passed it with a bow. Jessop took it, read the few lines of polite introduction, put it down. He looked appraisingly at his visitor. A tall man, carrying himself rather stiffly, aged thirty or thereabouts. The fair hair was close cropped in the continental fashion. The stranger's speech was slow and careful with a very definite foreign intonation, though grammatically correct. He was, Jessop noticed, not at all nervous or unsure of himself. That in itself was unusual. Most of the people who came into this office were nervous or excited or apprehensive. Sometimes they were shifty, sometimes vehement.

This was a man who had complete command of himself, a man with a poker face who knew what he was doing and why, and who would not be easily tricked or betrayed into saying more than he meant to say. Jessop said pleasantly,

"And what can we do for you?"

"I came to ask if you had any further news of Thomas Betterton, who disappeared recently in what seems a somewhat sensational manner. One cannot, I know, believe exactly what one reads in the press, so I ask where I can go for reliable information. They tell me— *you.*"

"I'm sorry we've no definite information about Betterton."

"I thought perhaps he might have been sent abroad on some mission." He paused and added, rather quaintly, "You know, hush-hush."

"My dear sir." Jessop looked pained. "Betterton was a scientist, not a diplomat or a secret agent."

"I am rebuked. But labels are not always correct. You will want to inquire my interest in the matter. Thomas Betterton was a relation of mine by marriage."

"Yes. You are the nephew, I believe, of the late Professor Mannheim."

"Ah, that you knew already. You are well informed here."

"People come along and tell us things," murmured Jessop. "Betterton's wife was here. She told me. You had written to her."

"Yes, to express my condolences and to ask if she had had any further news."

"That was very correct."

"My mother was Professor Mannheim's only sister. They were much attached. In Warsaw when I was a child I was much at my uncle's house, and his daughter, Elsa, was to me like a sister. When my father and mother died my home was with my uncle and cousin. They were happy days. Then came the war, the tragedies, the horrors. . . . Of all that we will not speak. My uncle and Elsa escaped to America. I myself remained in the underground Resistance, and after the war ended I had certain assignments. One visit I paid to America to see my uncle and cousin, that was all. But there came a time when my commitments in Europe are ended. I intend to reside in the States permanently. I shall be, I hope, near my uncle and my cousin and her husband. But alas—" he spread out his hands, "—I get there and my uncle, he is dead, my cousin, too, and her husband he has come to this country and has married again. So once more I have no family. And then I read of the disappearance of the well-known scientist Thomas Betterton, and I come over to see what can be done." He paused and looked enquiringly at Jessop.

Jessop looked expressionlessly back at him.

"Why did he disappear, Mr. Jessop?"

"That," said Jessop pleasantly, "is just what we'd like to know."

"Perhaps you do know?"

Jessop appreciated with some interest how easily their roles might become reversed. In this room he was accustomed to ask questions of people. This stranger was not the inquisitor. Still smiling pleasantly, Jessop replied,

"I assure you we do not."

"But you suspect?"

"It is possible," said Jessop cautiously, "that the thing follows a certain pattern. . . . There have been occurrences of this kind before."

"I know." Rapidly the visitor cited a half dozen cases. "All scientists," he said, with significance.

"Yes."

"They have gone beyond the Iron Curtain?"

"It is a possibility, but we do not know."

"But they have gone of their own free will?"

"Even that," said Jessop, "is difficult to say."

"It is not my business you think?"

"Oh, please."

"But you are right. It is of interest to me only because of Betterton."

"You'll forgive me," said Jessop, "if I don't quite understand your interest. After all, Betterton is only a relation by marriage. You didn't even know him."

"That is true. But for us Poles, the family is very important. There are obligations." He stood up and bowed stiffly. "I regret that I have trespassed upon your time, and I thank you for your courtesy."

Jessop rose also.

"I'm sorry we cannot help you," he said, "but I assure you we are completely in the dark. If I do hear of anything can I reach you?"

"Care of the U.S. Embassy will find me. I thank you." Again he bowed formally.

Jessop touched the buzzer. Major Glydr went out. Jessop lifted the receiver.

"Ask Colonel Wharton to come to my room."

When Wharton entered the room Jessop said:

"Things are moving—at last."

"How?"

"Mrs. Betterton wants to go abroad."

Wharton whistled.

"Going to join hubby?"

"I'm hopeful. She came provided with a convenient letter from her medical adviser. Complete need of rest and change of scene."

"Looks good!"

"Though, of course, it may be true," Jessop warned him. "A simple statement of fact."

"We never take that view here," said Wharton.

"No. I must say she does her stuff very convincingly. Never slips up for a moment."

"You got nothing further from her, I suppose?"

"One faint lead. The Speeder woman with whom Betterton lunched at the Dorset."

"Yes?"

"He didn't tell his wife about the lunch."

"Oh," Wharton considered. "You think that's relevant?"

"It might be. Carol Speeder was up before the Committee for the investigation of un-American Activities. She cleared herself, but all the same . . . yes, all the same she was, or they thought she was, tarred with that brush. It *may* be a possible contact. The only one we've found for Betterton so far."

"What about Mrs. Betterton's contacts—any possible contact lately who could have instigated the going abroad business?"

"No personal contact. She had a letter yesterday from a Pole. A cousin of Betterton's first wife. I had him here just now asking for details, etc."

"What's he like?"

"Not real," said Jessop. "All very foreign and correct, got all the 'gen,' curiously unreal as a personality."

"Think he's been the contact to tip her off?"

"It could be. I don't know. He puzzles me."

"Going to keep tabs on him?"

Jessop smiled.

"Yes. I pressed the buzzer twice."

"You old spider—with your tricks." Wharton became businesslike again. "Well, what's the form?"

"Janet, I think, and the usual. Spain, or Morocco."

"Not Switzerland?"

"Not this time."

"I should have thought Spain or Morocco would have been difficult for them."

"We mustn't under-estimate our adversaries."

Wharton flipped the security files disgustedly with his nail.

"About the only two countries where Betterton *hasn't* been seen," he said with chagrin. "Well, we'll lay it all on. My God, if we fall down on the job this time—"

Jessop leaned back in his chair.

"It's a long time since I've had a holiday," he said. "I'm rather sick of this office. I *might* take a little trip abroad. . . ."

3

"FLIGHT 108 TO PARIS. Air France. This way please."

The persons in the lounge at Heathrow Airport rose to their feet. Hilary Craven picked up her small, lizard skin travelling case and moved in the wake of the others, out onto the tarmac. The wind blew sharply cold after the heated air of the lounge.

Hilary shivered and drew her furs a little closer round her. She followed the other passengers across to where the aircraft was waiting. This was it! She was off —escaping! Out of the greyness, the coldness, the dead numb misery. Escaping to sunshine and blue skies and a new life. She would leave all this weight behind, this dead weight of misery and frustration. She went up the gangway of her plane, bending her head as she passed inside and was shown by the steward to her seat. For the first time in months she savoured relief from a pain that had been so sharply acute as almost to be physical. "I shall get away," she said to herself, hopefully. "I *shall* get away."

The roaring and the revolutions of the plane excited her. There seemed a kind of elemental savagery in it. Civilized misery, she thought, is the worst misery. Grey and hopeless. "But now," she thought, "I shall escape."

The plane taxied gently along the runway. The air hostess said:

"Fasten your belts, please."

The plane made a half turn and stood waiting its signal to depart. Hilary thought, "Perhaps the plane

will crash. . . . Perhaps it will never rise off the ground.
Then that will be the end, that will be the solution to
everything." They seemed to wait for ages out on the
airfield. Waiting for the signal to start off to freedom,
Hilary thought, absurdly; "I shall never get away,
never. I shall be kept here—a prisoner. . . ."

Ah, at last.

A final roar of engines, then the plane started forward. Quicker, quicker, racing along. Hilary thought;
"It won't rise. It can't. . . . This is the end." Ah, they
were above the ground now, it seemed. Not so much
that the plane rose as that the earth was falling away,
dropping down, thrusting its problems and its disappointments and its frustrations beneath the soaring
creature rising up so proudly into the clouds. Up they
went, circling round, the aerodrome looking like a ridiculous child's toy beneath. Funny little roads, strange
little railways with toy trains on them. A ridiculous
childish world where people loved and hated and
broke their hearts. None of it mattered because
they were all so ridiculous and so pettily small and
unimportant. Now there were clouds below them, a
dense, greyish-white mass. They must be over the Chan-
nel now. Hilary leaned back, closing her eyes. Escape.
Escape. She had left England, left Nigel, left the sad
little mound that was Brenda's grave. All left behind.
She opened her eyes, closed them again with a long
sigh. She slept. . . .

2

When Hilary awoke, the plane was coming down.
"Paris," thought Hilary, as she sat up in her seat and
reached for her handbag. But it was not Paris. The air
hostess came down the car saying, with that nursery

governess brightness that some travellers found so an-
noying:

"We are landing you at Beauvais as the fog is very
thick in Paris."

The suggestion in her manner was: "Won't that be
nice, children?" Hilary peered down through the small
space of window at her side. She could see little. Beauvais also appeared to be wreathed in fog. The plane
was circling round slowly. It was some time before it
finally made its landing. Then the passengers were marshalled through cold, damp mist into a rough wooden
building with a few chairs and a long wooden counter.

Depression settled down on Hilary but she tried to
fight it off. A man near her murmured:

"An old war aerodrome. No heating or comforts here.
Still, fortunately being the French, they'll serve us out
some drinks."

True enough, almost immediately a man came along
with some keys and presently passengers were being
served with various forms of alcoholic refreshment to
boost their morale. It helped to buoy the passengers up
for the long and irritating wait.

Some hours passed before anything happened. Other
planes appeared out of the fog and landed, also diverted
from Paris. Soon the small room was crowded with cold,
irritable people grumbling about the delay.

To Hilary it all had an unreal quality. It was as
though she was still in a dream, mercifully protected
from contact with reality. This was only a delay, only
a matter of waiting. She was still on her journey—her
journey of escape. She was still getting away from it
all, still going towards that spot where her life would
start again. Her mood held. Held through the long,
fatiguing delay, held through the moments of chaos
when it was announced, long after dark, that buses had
come to convey the travellers to Paris.

There was then a wild confusion, of coming and going, passengers, officials, porters all carrying baggage, hurrying and colliding in the darkness. In the end Hilary found herself, her feet and legs icy cold, in a bus slowly rumbling its way through the fog towards Paris.

It was a long weary drive taking four hours. It was midnight when they arrived at the Invalides and Hilary was thankful to collect her baggage and drive to the hotel where accommodation was reserved for her. She was too tired to eat—just had a hot bath and tumbled into bed.

The plane to Casablanca was due to leave Orly Airport at ten thirty the following morning, but when they arrived at Orly everything was confusion. Planes had been grounded in many parts of Europe, arrivals had been delayed as well as departures.

A harassed clerk at the departure desk shrugged his shoulders and said:

"Impossible for Madame to go on the flight where she had reservations! The schedules have all had to be changed. If Madame will take a seat for a little minute, presumably all will arrange itself." In the end she was summoned and told that there was a place on a plane going to Dakar which normally did not touch down at Casablanca but would do so on this occasion.

"You will arrive three hours later, that is all, Madame, on this later service."

Hilary acquiesced without protest and the official seemed surprised and positively delighted by her attitude.

"Madame has no conceptions of the difficulties that have been made to me this morning," he said. *"Enfin,* they are unreasonable, Messieurs the travellers. It is not I who made the fog! Naturally it has caused the disruptions. One must accommodate oneself with the good humour—that is what I say, however displeasing it is to have one's plans altered. *Après tout,* Madame, a little delay of an hour or two hours or three hours, what does it matter? How can it matter by what plane one arrives at Casablanca?"

Yet on that particular day it mattered more than the little Frenchman knew when he spoke those words. For when Hilary finally arrived and stepped out into the sunshine on to the tarmac, the porter who was moving beside her with his piled-up trolley of luggage observed:

"You have the lucky chance, Madame, not to have been on the plane before this, the regular plane for Casablanca."

Hilary said: "Why, what happened?"

The man looked uneasily to and fro, but after all, the news could not be kept secret. He lowered his voice confidentially and leant towards her.

"Mauvaise affaire!" he muttered. "It crashed—landing. The pilot and the navigator are dead and most of the passengers. Four or five were alive and have been taken to hospital. Some of those are badly hurt."

Hilary's first reaction was a kind of blinding anger. Almost unprompted there leapt into her mind the thought, "Why wasn't *I* in that plane? If I had been it would have been all over now—I should be dead, out of it all. No more heartaches, no more misery. The people in that plane wanted to live. And I—I don't care. Why shouldn't it have been me?"

She passed through the Customs, a perfunctory affair, and drove with her baggage to the hotel. It was a glorious, sunlit afternoon, with the sun just sinking to rest. The clear air and golden light—it was all as she had pictured it. She had arrived! She had left the fog, the cold, the darkness of London; she had left behind her misery and indecision and suffering. Here there was pulsating life and colour and sunshine.

She crossed her bedroom and threw open the shut-

ters, looking out into the street. Yes, it was all as she
had pictured it would be. Hilary turned slowly away
from the window and sat down on the side of the bed.
Escape, escape! That was the refrain that had hummed
incessantly in her mind ever since she left England.
Escape. Escape. And now she knew—knew with a horrible, stricken coldness, *that there was no escape.*

Everything was just the same here as it had been in
London. She herself, Hilary Craven, was the same. It
was from Hilary Craven that she was trying to escape,
and Hilary Craven was Hilary Craven in Morocco just
as much as she had been Hilary Craven in London.
She said very softly to herself:

"What a fool I've been—what a fool I *am*. Why did
I think that I'd feel differently if I got away from England?"

Brenda's grave, that small pathetic mound, was in
England and Nigel would shortly be marrying his new
wife, in England. Why had she imagined that those
two things would matter less to her here? Wishful
thinking, that was all. Well, that was all over now. She
was up against reality. The reality of herself and what
she could bear, and what she could *not* bear. One could
bear things, Hilary thought, so long as there was a
reason for bearing them. She had borne her own long
illness, she had borne Nigel's defection and the cruel
and brutal circumstances in which it had operated.
She had borne these things because there was Brenda.
Then had come the long, slow, losing fight for Brenda's
life—the final defeat. . . . Now there was nothing to
live for any longer. It had taken the journey to Morocco
to prove that to her. In London she had had a queer,
confused feeling that if only she could get somewhere
else she could forget what lay behind her and start
again. And so she had booked her journey to this place
which had no associations with the past, a place quite

new to her which had the qualities she loved so much: sunlight, pure air and the strangeness of new people and things. Here, she had thought, things will be different. But they were not different. They were the same. The facts were quite simple and unescapable. She, Hilary Craven, had no longer any wish to go on living. It was as simple as that.

If the fog had not intervened, if she had travelled on the plane on which her reservations had been made, then her problem might have been solved by now. She might be lying now in some French official mortuary, a body broken and battered with her spirit at peace, freed from suffering. Well, the same end could be achieved, but she would have to take a little trouble.

It would have been so easy if she had had sleeping stuff with her. She remembered how she had asked Dr. Grey and the rather queer look on his face as he had answered:

"Better not. Much better to learn to sleep naturally. May be hard at first, but it will come."

A queer look on his face. Had he known then or suspected that it would come to this? Oh well, it should not be difficult. She rose to her feet with decision. She would go out now to a chemist's shop.

3

Hilary had always imagined that drugs were easy to buy in foreign cities. Rather to her surprise, she found that this was not so. The chemist she went to first supplied her with only two doses. For more than that amount, he said, a doctor's prescription would be advisable. She thanked him smilingly and nonchalantly and went rather quickly out of the shop, colliding as she did so with a tall, rather solemn-faced young man, who apologized in English. She heard him asking for toothpaste as she left the shop.

Somehow that amused her. Toothpaste. It seemed so ridiculous, so normal, so everyday. Then a sharp pang pierced her, for the toothpaste he had asked for was the brand that Nigel had always preferred. She crossed the street and went into a shop opposite. She had been to four chemist's shops by the time she returned to the hotel. It had amused her a little that in the third shop the owlish young man had again appeared, once more asking obstinately for his particular brand of toothpaste which evidently was not one commonly stocked by French chemists in Casablanca.

Hilary felt almost lighthearted as she changed her frock and made up her face before going down for dinner. She purposely went down as late as possible since she was anxious not to encounter any of her fellow travellers or the *personnel* of the aeroplane. That was hardly likely in any case, since the plane had gone on to Dakar, she thought that she had been the only person put off at Casablanca.

The restaurant was almost empty by the time she came into it, though she noticed that the young Englishman with the owl-like face was just finishing his meal at the table by the wall. He was reading a French newspaper and seemed quite absorbed in it.

Hilary ordered herself a good meal with a half bottle of wine. She was feeling a heady kind of excitement. She thought to herself, "What is this after all, but the last adventure?" Then she ordered a bottle of Vichy water to be sent up to her room and went straight up after leaving the dining room.

The waiter brought the Vichy, uncapped it, placed it on the table, and wishing her goodnight, left the room. Hilary drew a sigh of relief. As he closed the door after him, she went to it and turned the key in the lock.

"Funny," he said. "I came to ask you that." He gave a quick sideways nod toward the preparations on the table. Hilary said sharply:

"I don't know what you mean."

"Oh yes, you do."

Hilary paused, struggling for words. There were so many things she wanted to say. To express indignation. To order him out of the room. But strangely enough, it was curiosity that won the day. The question rose to her lips so naturally that she was almost unaware of asking it.

"That key," she said, "it turned, of itself, in the lock?"

"Oh, that!" The young man gave a sudden boyish grin that transformed his face. He put his hand into his pocket, and taking out a metal instrument, he handed it to her to examine.

"There you are," he said, "very handy little tool. Insert it into the lock the other side, it grips the key and turns it." He took it back from her and put it in his pocket. "Burglars use them," he said.

"So you're a burglar?"

"No, no, Mrs. Craven, do me justice. I did knock, you know. Burglars don't knock. Then, when it seemed you weren't going to let me in, I used this."

"But why?"

Again her visitor's eyes strayed to the preparations on the table.

"I shouldn't do it if I were you," he said. "It isn't a bit what you think, you know. You think you just go to sleep and you don't wake up. But it's not quite like that. All sorts of unpleasant effects. Convulsions sometimes, gangrene of the skin. If you're resistant to the drug, it takes a long time to work, and someone gets to you in time and then all sorts of unpleasant things happen. Stomach pump. Castor oil, hot coffee, slapping and pushing. All very undignified, I assure you."

Hilary leaned back in her chair, her eyelids narrowed. She clenched her hands slightly. She forced herself to smile.

"What a ridiculous person you are," she said. "Do you imagine that I was committing suicide, or something like that?"

"Not only imagine it," said the young man called Jessop, "I'm quite sure of it. I was in that chemist, you know, when you came in. Buying toothpaste, as a matter of fact. Well, they hadn't got the sort I like, so I went to another shop. And there you were, asking for sleeping pills again. Well, I thought that a bit odd, you know, so I followed you. All those sleeping pills at different places. It could only add up to one thing."

His tone was friendly, offhand, but quite assured. Looking at him Hilary Craven abandoned pretence.

"Then don't you think it is unwarrantable impertinence on your part to try and stop me?"

He considered the point for a moment or two. Then he shook his head.

"No. It's one of those things that you can't *not* do—if you understand."

Hilary spoke with energy. "You can stop me for the moment. I mean you can take the pills away—throw them out of the window or something like that—but you can't stop me from buying more another day or throwing myself down from the top floor of the building, or jumping in front of a train."

The young man considered this.

"No," he said. "I agree I can't stop you doing any of those things. But it's a question, you know, whether you will do them. Tomorrow, that is."

"You think I shall feel differently tomorrow?" asked Hilary, faint bitterness in her tone.

"People do," said Jessop, almost apologetically.

"Yes, perhaps," she considered. "If you're doing

things in a mood of hot despair. But when it's cold despair, it's different. I've nothing to live for, you see."

Jessop put his rather owlish head on one side, and blinked.

"Interesting," he remarked.

"Not really. Not interesting at all. I'm not a very interesting woman. My husband, whom I loved, left me, my only child died very painfully of meningitis. I've no near friends or relations. I've no vocation, no art or craft or work that I love doing."

"Tough," said Jessop appreciatively. He added, rather hesitantly: "You don't think of it as—wrong?"

Hilary said heatedly: "Why should it be wrong? It's *my* life."

"Oh yes, yes," Jessop repeated hastily. "I'm not taking a high moral line myself, but there *are* people, you know, who think it's wrong."

Hilary said,

"I'm not one of them."

Mr. Jessop said, rather inadequately,

"Quite."

He sat there looking at her, blinking his eyes thoughtfully. Hilary said:

"So perhaps now, Mr.—er—"

"Jessop," said the young man.

"So perhaps now, Mr. Jessop, you will leave me alone."

But Jessop shook his head.

"Not just yet," he said. "I wanted to know, you see, just what was behind it all. I've got it clear now, have I? You're not interested in life, you don't want to live any longer, you more or less welcome the idea of death?"

"Yes."

"Good," said Jessop, cheerfully. "So now we know

where we are. Let's go on to the next step. Has it *got* to be sleeping pills?"

"What do you mean?"

"Well, I've already told you that they're not as romantic as they sound. Throwing yourself off a building isn't too nice, either. You don't always die at once. And the same applies to falling under a train. What I'm getting at is that there *are* other ways."

"I don't understand what you mean."

"I'm suggesting another method. Rather a sporting method, really. There's some excitement in it, too. I'll be fair with you. There's just a hundred to one chance that you mightn't die. But I don't believe under the circumstances, that you'd really object by that time."

"I haven't the faintest idea what you're talking about."

"Of course you haven't," said Jessop. "I've not begun to tell you about it yet. I'm afraid I'll have to make rather a thing about it—tell you a story, I mean. Shall I go ahead?"

"I suppose so."

Jessop paid no attention to the grudgingness of the assent. He started off in his most owl-like manner.

"You're the sort of woman who reads the papers and keeps up with things generally, I expect," he said. "You'll have read about the disappearance of various scientists from time to time. There was that Italian chap about a year ago, and about two months ago a young scientist called Thomas Betterton disappeared."

Hilary nodded. "Yes, I read about that in the papers."

"Well, there's been a good deal more than has appeared in the papers. More people, I mean, have disappeared. They haven't always been scientists. Some of them have been young men who were engaged in important medical research. Some of them have been research chemists, some of them have been physicists, there was one barrister. Oh, quite a lot here and there and everywhere. Well, ours is a so-called free country. You can leave it if you like. But in these peculiar circumstances we've got to know why these people left it and where they went, and, also important, *how* they went. Did they go of their own free will? Were they kidnapped? Were they blackmailed into going? What route did they take—what kind of organisation is it that sets this in motion and what is its ultimate aim? Lots of questions. We want the answer to them. You might be able to help get us that answer."

Hilary stared at him.

"Me? How? Why?"

"I'm coming down to the particular case of Thomas Betterton. He disappeared from Paris just over two months ago. He left a wife in England. She was distracted—or said she was distracted. She swore that she had no idea why he'd gone or where or how. That may be true, or it may not. Some people—and I'm one of them—think it wasn't true."

Hilary leaned forward in her chair. In spite of herself she was becoming interested. Jessop went on.

"We prepared to keep a nice, unobstrusive eye on Mrs. Betterton. About a fortnight ago she came to me and told me she had been ordered by her doctor to go abroad, take a thorough rest and get some distraction. She was doing no good in England, and people were continually bothering her—newspaper reporters, relations, kind friends."

Hilary said drily: "I can imagine it."

"Yes, tough. Quite natural she would want to get away for a bit."

"Quite natural, I should think."

"But we've got nasty, suspicious minds in our department, you know. We arranged to keep tabs on Mrs.

Betterton. Yesterday she left England as arranged, for Casablanca."

"Casablanca?"

"Yes—*en route* to other places in Morocco, of course. All quite open and above board, plans made, bookings ahead. But it may be that this trip to Morocco is where Mrs. Betterton steps off into the unknown."

Hilary shrugged her shoulders.

"I don't see where I come in to all this."

Jessop smiled.

"You come into it because you've got a very magnificent head of red hair, Mrs. Craven."

"Hair?"

"Yes. It's the most noticeable thing about Mrs. Betterton—her hair. You've heard, perhaps, that the plane before yours today crashed on landing."

"I know. I should have been on that plane. I actually had reservations for it."

"Interesting," said Jessop. "Well, Mrs. Betterton *was* on that plane. She wasn't killed. She was taken out of the wreckage still alive, and she is in hospital now. But according to the doctor, she won't be alive tomorrow morning."

A faint glimmer of light came to Hilary. She looked at him enquiringly.

"Yes," said Jessop, "perhaps now you see the form of suicide I'm offering you. I'm suggesting that Mrs. Betterton goes on with her journey. I'm suggesting that you should become Mrs. Betterton."

"But surely," said Hilary, "that would be quite impossible. I mean, they'd know at once she wasn't me."

Jessop put his head on one side.

"That, of course, depends entirely on whom you mean by 'they.' It's a very vague term. Who is or are 'they'? Is there such a thing, are there such persons as 'they'? We don't know. But I can tell you this. If the most popular explanation of 'they' is accepted, then these people work in very close, self-contained cells. They do that for their own security. If Mrs. Betterton's journey had a purpose and is planned, then the people who were in charge of it here will know nothing about the English side of it. At the appointed moment they will contact a certain woman at a certain place, and carry on from there. Mrs. Betterton's passport description is five-feet-seven, red hair, blue eyes, mouth medium, no distinguishing marks. Good enough."

"But the authorities here. Surely they—"

Jessop smiled. "That part of it will be quite all right. The French have lost a few valuable young scientists and chemists of their own. They'll co-operate. The facts will be as follows. Mrs. Betterton, suffering from concussion, is taken to hospital. Mrs. Craven, another passenger in the crashed plane will also be admitted to hospital. Within a day or two *Mrs. Craven will die in hospital,* and Mrs. Betterton will be discharged, suffering slightly from concussion, but able to proceed on her tour. The crash was genuine, the concussion is genuine, and concussion makes a very good cover for you. It excuses a lot of things like lapses of memory and various unpredictable behaviour."

Hilary said:

"It would be madness!"

"Oh, yes," said Jessop, "it's madness, all right. It's a very tough assignment and if our suspicions are realised, you'll probably cop it. You see, I'm being quite frank, but according to you, you're prepared and anxious to cop it. As an alternative to throwing yourself in front of a train or something like that, I should think you'd find it far more amusing."

Suddenly and unexpectedly Hilary laughed.

"I do believe," she said, "that you're quite right."

"You'll do it?"

"Yes. Why not?"

"In that case," said Jessop, rising in his seat with sudden energy, "there's absolutely no time to be lost."

4

IT WAS NOT REALLY COLD in the hospital but it felt cold. There was a smell of antiseptics in the air. Occasionally in the corridor outside could be heard the rattle of glasses and instruments as a trolley was pushed by. Hilary Craven sat in a hard iron chair by a bedside.

In the bed, lying flat under a shaded light with her head bandaged, Olive Betterton lay unconscious. There was a nurse standing on one side of the bed and the doctor on the other. Jessop sat in a chair in the far corner of the room. The doctor turned to him and spoke in French.

"It will not be very long now," he said. "The pulse is very much weaker."

"And she will not recover consciousness?"

The Frenchman shrugged his shoulders.

"That I cannot say. It may be, yes, at the very end."

"There is nothing you can do—no stimulant?"

The doctor shook his head. He went out. The nurse followed him. She was replaced by a nun who moved to the head of the bed, and stood there, fingering her rosary. Hilary looked at Jessop and in obedience to a glance from him came to join him.

"You heard what the doctor said?" he asked in a low voice.

"Yes. What is it you want to say to her?"

"If she regains consciousness I want any information you can possibly get, any password, any sign, any mes-

51

sage, *anything*. Do you understand? She is more likely to speak to you than to me."

Hilary said with sudden emotion:

"You want me to betray someone who is dying?"

Jessop put his head on one side in the birdlike manner which he sometimes adopted.

"So it seems like that to you, does it?" he said, considering.

"Yes, it does."

He looked at her thoughtfully.

"Very well then, you shall say and do what you please. For myself I can have no scruples! You understand that?"

"Of course. It's your duty. You'll do whatever questioning you please, but don't ask *me* to do it."

"You're a free agent."

"There is one question we shall have to decide. Are we to tell her that she is dying?"

"I don't know. I shall have to think it out."

She nodded and went back to her place by the bed. She was filled now with a deep compassion for the woman who lay there dying. The woman who was on her way to join the man she loved. Or were they all wrong? Had she come to Morocco simply to seek solace, to pass the time until perhaps some definite news could come to her as to whether her husband were alive or dead? Hilary wondered.

Time went on. It was nearly two hours later when the click of the nun's beads stopped. She spoke in a soft impersonal voice.

"There is a change," she said. "I think, Madame, it is the end that comes. I will fetch the doctor."

She left the room. Jessop moved to the opposite side of the bed, standing back against the wall so that he was out of the woman's range of vision. The eyelids flickered and opened. Pale incurious blue eyes looked into Hilary's. They closed, then opened again. A faint air of perplexity seemed to come into them.

"Where . . . ?"

The word fluttered between the almost breathless lips, just as the doctor entered the room. He took her hand in his, his finger on the pulse, standing by the bed looking down on her.

"You are in hospital, Madame," he said. "There was an accident to the plane."

"To the plane?"

The words were repeated dreamily in that faint breathless voice.

"Is there anyone you want to see in Casablanca, Madame? Any message we can take?"

Her eyes were raised painfully to the doctor's face. She said:

"No."

She looked back again at Hilary.

"Who—who—"

Hilary bent forward and spoke clearly and distinctly.

"I came out from England on a plane, too—if there is anything I can do to help you, please tell me."

"No—nothing—nothing—unless—"

"Yes?"

"Nothing."

The eyes flickered again and half closed—Hilary raised her head and looked across to meet Jessop's imperious commanding glance. Firmly, she shook her head.

Jessop moved forward. He stood close beside the doctor. The dying woman's eyes opened again. Sudden recognition came into them. She said:

"I know *you*."

"Yes, Mrs. Betterton, you know me. Will you tell me anything you can about your husband?"

"No."

Her eyelids fell again. Jessop turned quietly and left the room. The doctor looked across at Hilary. He said very softly,

"*C'est la fin!*"

The dying woman's eyes opened again. They travelled painfully round the room, then they remained fixed on Hilary. Olive Betterton made a very faint motion with her hand, and Hilary instinctively took the white cold hand between her own. The doctor, with a shrug of his shoulders and a little bow, left the room. The two women were alone together. Olive Betterton was trying to speak:

"Tell me—tell me—"

Hilary knew what she was asking, and suddenly her own course of action opened clearly before her. She leaned down over the recumbent form.

"Yes," she said, her words clear and emphatic. "You are dying. That's what you want to know, isn't it? Now listen to me. I am going to try and reach your husband. Is there any message you want me to give him if I succeed?"

"Tell him—tell him—to be careful. Boris—Boris—dangerous. . . ."

The breath fluttered off again with a sigh. Hilary bent closer.

"Is there anything you can tell me to help me—help me in my journey, I mean? Help me to get in contact with your husband?"

"*Snow.*"

The word came so faintly that Hilary was puzzled. Snow? *Snow?* She repeated it uncomprehendingly. A faint, ghost-like little giggle came from Olive Betterton. Faint words came tumbling out:

> "*Snow, snow, beautiful snow!*
> *You slip on a lump, and over you go!*"

She repeated the last word. "Go . . . Go? Go and tell him about Boris. I didn't believe it. I *wouldn't* believe it. But perhaps it's true. . . . If so, if so . . ." a kind of agonised question came into her eyes which stared up into Hilary's. ". . . take care. . . ."

A queer little rattle came to her throat. Her lips jerked.

Olive Betterton died.

2

The next five days were strenuous mentally, though inactive physically. Immured in a private room in the hospital, Hilary was set to work. Every evening she had to pass an examination on what she had studied that day. All the details of Olive Betterton's life, as far as they could be ascertained, were set down on paper and she had to memorise and learn them by heart. The house she had lived in, the daily women she had employed, her relations, the names of her pet dog and her canary, every detail of the six months of her married life with Thomas Betterton. Her wedding, the names of her bridesmaids, their dresses, the patterns of the curtains, carpets and chintzes. Olive Betterton's tastes, predilections and day by day activities. Her preferences in food and drink. Hilary was forced to marvel at the amount of seemingly meaningless information that had been massed together. Once she said to Jessop:

"Can any of this possibly *matter?*"

And to that he had replied quietly:

"Probably not. But you've got to make yourself into the authentic article. Think of it this way, Hilary. You're a writer. You're writing a book about a woman. The woman is Olive. You describe scenes of her childhood, her girlhood; you describe her marriage, the house she lived in. All the time that you do it she becomes more and more of a real person to you. Then you go over it a second time. You write it this time as an autobiography. You write it *in the first person*. Do you see what I mean?"

She nodded slowly, impressed in spite of herself.

"You can't think of yourself as Olive Betterton until you *are* Olive Betterton. It would be better if you had time to learn it up, but *we can't afford time*. So I've got to cram you. Cram you like a schoolboy—like a student who is going in for an important examination." He added, "You've got a quick brain and a good memory, thank the Lord."

He looked at her in cool appraisement.

The passport descriptions of Olive Betterton and Hilary Craven were almost identical, but actually the two faces were entirely different. Olive Betterton had had a quality of rather commonplace and insignificant prettiness. She had looked obstinate but not intelligent. Hilary's face had power and an intriguing quality. The deep set bluish-green eyes under dark level brows had fire and intelligence in their depths. Her mouth curved upwards in a wide and generous line. The plane of the jaw was unusual—a sculptor would have found the angles of the face interesting.

Jessop thought: "There's passion there—and guts—and somewhere, damped but not quenched, there's a gay spirit that's tough—and that enjoys life and searches out for adventure."

"You'll do," he said to her. "You're an apt pupil."

This challenge to her intellect and her memory had stimulated Hilary. She was becoming interested now, keen to achieve success. Once or twice objections occurred to her. She voiced them to Jessop.

"You say that I shan't be rejected as Olive Betterton.

You say that they won't know what she looks like, except in general detail. But how sure can you be of that?"

Jessop shrugged his shoulders.

"One can't be sure—of anything. But we do know a certain amount about the set up of these shows, and it does seem that internationally there is very little communication from one country to another. Actually, that's a great advantage to *them*. If we come upon a weak link in England (and, mind you, in every organisation there always will be a weak link), that weak link in the chain knows nothing about what's going on in France, or Italy, or Germany, or wherever you like, we are brought up short by a blank wall. They know their own little part of the whole—no more. The same applies the opposite way round. I dare swear that all the cell operating here knows is that Olive Betterton will arrive on such and such a plane and is to be given such and such instructions. You see, it's not as though she were important in *herself*. If they're bringing her to her husband, it's because her husband wants her brought to him and because they think they'll get better work out of him if she joins him. She herself is a mere pawn in the game. You must remember too, that the idea of substituting a false Olive Betterton is definitely a spur of the moment improvisation—occasioned by the plane accident and the color of your hair. Our plan of operation was to keep tabs on Olive Betterton and find out where she went, *how* she went, whom she met—and so on. That's what the other side will be on the lookout for."

Hilary asked:

"Haven't you tried all that before?"

"Yes. It was tried in Switzerland. Very unobtrusively. And it failed as far as our main objective was concerned. *If* anyone contacted her there we didn't know about it. So the contact must have been very brief. Naturally they'll expect that someone will be keeping tabs on Olive Betterton. They'll be prepared for that. It's up to us to do our job more thoroughly than last time. We've got to try and be rather more cunning than our adversaries."

"So you'll be keeping tabs on me?"

"Of course."

"How?"

He shook his head.

"I shan't tell you that. Much better for you not to know. What you don't know you can't give away."

"Do you think I would give it away?"

Jessop put on his owl-like expression again.

"I don't know how good an actress you are—how good a liar. It's not easy, you know. It's not a question of *saying* anything indiscreet. It can be anything, a sudden intake of breath, the momentary pause in some action—lighting a cigarette, for instance. Recognition of a name or a friend. You could cover it up quickly, but just a flash might be enough!"

"I see. It means—being on your guard for every single split second."

"Exactly. In the meantime, on with the lessons! Quite like going back to school, isn't it? You're pretty well-word perfect on Olive Betterton, now. Let's go on to the other."

Codes, responses, various properties. The lesson went on, the questioning, the repetition, the endeavour to confuse her, to trip her up; then hypothetical schemes and her own reactions to them. In the end, Jessop nodded his head and declared himself satisfied.

"You'll do," he said. He patted her on the shoulder in an avuncular manner. "You're an apt pupil. And remember this, however much you may feel at times that you're all alone in this, you're probably not. I say *probably*—I won't put it higher than that. These are clever devils."

"What happens," said Hilary, "if I reach journey's end?"

"You mean?"

"I mean when at last I come face to face with Tom Betterton."

Jessop nodded grimly.

"Yes," he said. "That's the danger moment. I can only say that at that moment, *if all has gone well,* you *should* have protection. If, that is to say, things have gone as we *hope;* but the very basis of this operation, as you may remember, was that there wasn't a very high chance of survival."

"Didn't you say one in a hundred?" said Hilary drily.

"I think we can shorten the odds a little. I didn't know what you were like."

"No, I suppose not." She was thoughtful. "To you, I suppose, I was just . . ."

He finished the sentence for her:

"A woman with a noticeable head of red hair and who hadn't the pluck to go on living."

She flushed.

"That's a harsh judgement."

"It's a true one, isn't it? I don't go in for being sorry for people. For one thing it's insulting. One is only sorry for people when they're sorry for themselves. Self-pity is one of the biggest stumbling blocks in the world today."

Hilary said thoughtfully:

"I think perhaps you're right. Will you permit yourself to be sorry for me when I've been liquidated or whatever the term is, in fulfilling this mission?"

"Sorry for you? No. I shall curse like hell because we've lost someone who's worth while taking a bit of trouble over."

"A compliment at last." In spite of herself she was pleased.

She went on in a practical tone:

"There's just one other thing that occurred to me. You say nobody's likely to know what Olive Betterton looks like, but what about being recognised as *myself*? I don't know anyone in Casablanca, but there are the people who travelled here with me in the plane. Or one may of course run across somebody one knows among the tourists here."

"You needn't worry about the passengers in the plane. The people who flew with you from Paris were business men who went on to Dakar and a man who got off here who has since flown back to Paris. You will go to a different hotel when you leave here, the hotel for which Mrs. Betterton had reservations. You will be wearing her clothes and her style of hairdressing and one or two strips of plaster at the side of your face will make you look very different in feature. We've got a doctor coming to work upon you, by the way. Local anaesthetic, so it won't hurt, but you will have to have a few genuine marks of the accident."

"You're very thorough," said Hilary.

"Have to be."

"You've never asked me," said Hilary, "whether Olive Betterton told me anything before she died."

"I understood you had scruples."

"I'm sorry."

"Not at all. I respect you for them. I'd like to indulge in them myself—but they're not in the schedule."

"She did say something that perhaps I ought to tell you. She said 'Tell him'—Betterton, that is—'tell him to be careful—Boris—dangerous—' "

"Boris." Jessop repeated the name with interest. "Ah! Our correct foreign Major Boris Glydr."

"You know him? Who is he?"

"A Pole. He came to see me in London. He's supposed to be a cousin of Tom Betterton by marriage."

"Supposed?"

"Let us say, more correctly, that if he is who he says he is, he is a cousin of the late Mrs. Betterton. But we've only his word for it."

"She was frightened," said Hilary, frowning. "Can you describe him? I'd like to be able to recognise him."

"Yes. It might be as well. Six foot. Weight roughly 160 lbs. Fair—rather wooden poker face—light eyes—foreign stilted manner—English very correct, but a pronounced accent, military bearing."

He added:

"I had him tailed when he left my office. Nothing doing. He went straight to the U.S. Embassy—quite correctly—he'd brought me an introductory letter from there. The usual kind they send out when they want to be polite but non-committal. I presume he left the Embassy either in somebody's car or by the back entrance disguised as a footman or something. Anyway he evaded us. Yes—I should say that Olive Betterton was perhaps right when she said that Boris Glydr was dangerous."

5

IN THE SMALL FORMAL SALON of the Hotel St. Louis, three ladies were sitting, each engaged in her particular occupation. Mrs. Calvin Baker, short, plump, with well blued hair, was writing letters with the same driving energy she applied to all forms of activity. No one could have mistaken Mrs. Calvin Baker for anything but a travelling American, comfortably off, with an inexhaustible thirst for precise information on every subject under the sun.

In an uncomfortable Empire type chair, Miss Hetherington who again could not have been mistaken for anything but travelling English, was knitting one of those melancholy shapeless looking garments that English ladies of middle age always seem to be knitting. Miss Hetherington was tall and thin with a scraggy neck, badly arranged hair, and a general expression of moral disapprovement of the Universe.

Mademoiselle Jeanne Maricot was sitting gracefully in an upright chair, looking out of the window and yawning. Mademoiselle Maricot was a brunette dyed blonde, with a plain but excitingly made-up face. She was wearing chic clothes and had no interest whatsoever in the other occupants of the room whom she dismissed contemptuously in her mind as being exactly what they were! She was contemplating an important change in her sex life and had no interest to spare for these animals of tourists!

Miss Hetherington and Mrs. Calvin Baker, having

both spent a couple of nights under the roof of the St. Louis, had become acquainted. Mrs. Calvin Baker, with American friendliness, talked to everybody. Miss Hetherington, though just as eager for companionship, talked only to English and Americans of what she considered a certain social standing. The French she had no truck with unless guaranteed of respectable family life as evidenced by little ones who shared the parental table in the dining room.

A Frenchman looking like a prosperous business man glanced into the salon, was intimidated by its air of female solidarity and went out again with a look of lingering regret at Mademoiselle Jeanne Maricot.

Miss Hetherington began to count stitches *sotto voce*. "Twenty-eight, twenty-nine—now what can I have— Oh, I see."

A tall woman with red hair looked into the room and hesitated a moment before going on down the passage towards the dining room.

Mrs. Calvin Baker and Miss Hetherington were immediately alert. Mrs. Baker slewed herself round from the writing table and spoke in a thrilled whisper.

"Did you happen to notice that woman with red hair who looked in, Miss Hetherington? They say she's the only survivor of that terrible plane crash last week."

"I saw her arrive this afternoon," said Miss Hetherington, dropping another stitch in her excitement. *"In an ambulance."*

"Straight from the hospital, so the Manager said. I wonder now if it was wise—to leave hospital so soon. She's had concussion, I believe."

"She's got strapping on her face, too—cut, perhaps, by the glass. What a mercy she wasn't burnt. Terrible injuries from burning in these air accidents, I believe."

"It just doesn't bear thinking about. Poor young

thing. I wonder if she had a husband with her and if he was killed?"

"I don't think so," Miss Hetherington shook her yellow grey head. "It said in the paper, one woman passenger."

"That's right. It gave her name, too. A Mrs. Beverly —no, Betterton, that was it."

"Betterton," said Miss Hetherington reflectively. "Now what does that remind me of? Betterton. In the papers. Oh dear, I'm sure that was the name."

"Tant pis pour Pierre," Mademoiselle Maricot said to herself. *"Il est vraiment insupportable! Mais le petit Jules, lui il est bien gentil. Et son père est tres bien placé dans les affaires. Enfin, je me decide!"*

And with long graceful steps Mademoiselle Maricot walked out of the small salon and out of the story.

2

Mrs. Thomas Betterton had left the hospital that afternoon five days after the accident. An ambulance had driven her to the Hotel St. Louis.

Looking pale and ill, her face strapped and bandaged, Mrs. Betterton was shown at once to the room reserved for her, a sympathetic manager hovering in attendance.

"What emotions you must have experienced, Madame!" he said, after enquiring tenderly as to whether the room reserved suited her, and turning on all the electric lights quite unnecessarily. "But what an escape! What a miracle! What good fortune. Only three survivors, I understand, and one of them in a critical condition still."

Hilary sank down on a chair wearily.

"Yes, indeed," she murmured. "I can hardly believe

it myself. Even now I can remember so little. The last twenty-four hours before the crash are still quite vague to me."

The manager nodded sympathetically.

"Ah, yes. That is the result of the concussion. That happened once to a sister of mine. She was in London in the war. A bomb came, she was knocked unconscious. But presently she gets up, she walks about London and she takes a train from the station of Euston and, *figurez-vous,* she wakes up at Liverpool and she cannot remember anything of the bomb, of going across London, of the train or of getting there! The last thing she remembers is hanging up her skirt in the wardrobe in London. Very curious these things, are they not?"

Hilary agreed that they were, indeed. The manager bowed and departed. Hilary got up and looked at herself in the glass. So imbued was she now with her new personality that she positively felt the weakness in her limbs which would be natural to one who had just come out of the hospital after a severe ordeal.

She had already enquired at the desk, but there had been no messages or letters for her there. The first steps in her new role had to be taken very much in the dark. Olive Betterton might perhaps have been told to ring a certain number or to contact a certain person at Casablanca. As to that there was no clue. All the knowledge she had to go on was Olive Betterton's passport, her Letter of Credit, and her book of Cook's tickets and reservations. These provided for two days in Casablanca, six days in Fez and five days in Marrakesh. These reservations were now, of course, out of date, and would have to be dealt with accordingly. The passport, the Letter of Credit and the accompanying Letter of Identification had been suitably dealt with. The photograph on the passport was now that of Hilary, the signature on the Letter of Credit was *Olive Betterton* in

Hilary's handwriting. Her credentials were all in order. Her task was to play her part adequately and to wait. Her master card must be the plane accident, and its resultant loss of memory and general haziness.

It had been a genuine accident and Olive Betterton had been genuinely on board the plane. The fact of concussion would adequately cover her failure to adopt any measures in which she might have been instructed. Bewildered, dazed, weak, Olive Betterton would await orders.

The natural thing to do would be to rest. Accordingly she lay down on the bed. For two hours she went over in her mind all that she had been taught. Olive's luggage had been destroyed in the plane. Hilary had a few things with her supplied at the hospital. She passed a comb through her hair, touched her lips with a lipstick and went down to the hotel dining room for dinner.

She was looked at, she noticed, with a certain amount of interest. There were several tables occupied by business men and these hardly vouchsafed a glance at her. But at other tables, clearly occupied by tourists, she was conscious of a murmur and a whisper going on.

"That woman over there—the one with the red hair —she's a survivor of the plane crash, my dear. Yes, came from hospital in an ambulance. I saw her arrive. She looks terribly ill still. I wonder if they ought to have let her out so soon. What a frightful experience. What a merciful escape!"

After dinner Hilary sat for a short while in the small formal salon. She wondered if anyone would approach her in any way. There were one or two other women scattered about the room, and presently a small, plump, middle-aged woman with well-blued white hair, moved to a chair near hers. She opened proceedings in a brisk, pleasant American voice.

"I do hope you'll excuse me, but I just felt I had to say a word. It's you, isn't it, who had the *wonderful* escape from that air crash the other day?"

Hilary put down the magazine she was reading.

"Yes," she said.

"My! Isn't that terrible? The crash I mean. Only three survivors, they say. Is that right?"

"Only two," said Hilary. "One of the three died in hospital."

"My! You don't say. Now, if you don't mind my asking, Miss—Mrs. . . . ."

"Betterton."

"Well, if you don't mind my asking, just where were you sitting in that plane? Were you up at the front or near the tail?"

Hilary knew the answer to that one and gave it promptly.

"Near the tail."

"They always say, don't they, that's the safest place. I just insist now on always having a place near the rear doors. Did you hear that, Miss Hetherington?" She turned her head to include another middle-aged lady. This one was uncompromisingly British with a long, sad, horselike face. "It's just as I was saying the other day. Whenever you go into an aeroplane, don't you let those air hostesses take you right up to the front."

"I suppose someone has to sit at the front," said Hilary.

"Well, it won't be me," said her new American friend promptly. "My name's Baker, by the way, Mrs. Calvin Baker."

Hilary acknowledged the introduction and Mrs. Baker plunged on, monopolising the conversation easily.

"I've just come here from Mogador and Miss Hetherington has come from Tangier. We became acquainted

here. Are you going to visit Marrakesh, Mrs. Betterton?"

"I'd arranged to do so," said Hilary. "Of course, this
accident has thrown out all my time schedule."

"Why, naturally, I can see that. But you really
mustn't miss Marrakesh, wouldn't you say so, Miss
Hetherington?"

"Marrakesh is terribly expensive," said Miss Hetherington. "This miserable travel allowance makes everything so difficult."

"There's a wonderful hotel, the Mamounia," continued Mrs. Baker.

"Wickedly expensive," said Miss Hetherington. "Out
of the question for *me*. Of course, it's different for you,
Mrs. Baker—dollars, I mean. But someone gave me the
name of a small hotel there, really very nice and clean,
and the food, they say, is not at all bad."

"Where else do you plan to go, Mrs. Betterton?"
asked Mrs. Calvin Baker.

"I would like to see Fez," said Hilary, cautiously. "I
shall have to get fresh reservations, of course."

"Oh, yes, you certainly oughtn't to miss Fez or Rabat."

"You've been there?"

"Not yet. I'm planning to go there shortly, and so is
Miss Hetherington."

"I believe the old city is quite unspoilt," said Miss
Hetherington.

The conversation continued in desultory fashion for
some time further. Then Hilary pleaded fatigue from
her first day out of the hospital and went up to her bedroom.

The evening so far had been quite indecisive. The
two women who had talked to her had been such well-
known travelling types that she could hardly believe that
they were other than they seemed. Tomorrow, she de-

cided, if she had received no word or communication of any kind, she would go to Cook's and raise the question of fresh reservations at Fez and Marrakesh.

There were no letters, messages or telephone calls the following morning and about eleven o'clock she made her way to the travel agency. There was somewhat of a queue, but when she at last reached the counter and began talking to the clerk, an interruption occurred. A somewhat more senior clerk with glasses elbowed the young man aside. He beamed at Hilary through his glasses.

"It is Madame Betterton, is it not? I have all your reservations made."

"I am afraid," said Hilary, "that they will be out of date. I have been in hospital and . . ."

"Ah, *mais oui*, I know all that. Let me congratulate you on your escape, Madame. But I got your telephone message about fresh reservations, and we have them here ready for you."

Hilary felt a faint quickening of her pulse. As far as she knew no one had phoned the travel agency. Here then were definite signs that Olive Betterton's travelling arrangements were being supervised. She said,

"I wasn't sure if they had telephoned or not."

"But yes, Madame. Here, I will show you."

He produced railway tickets, and vouchers for hotel accommodation, and a few minutes later the transactions were completed. Hilary was to leave for Fez on the following day.

Mrs. Calvin Baker was not in the restaurant either for lunch or dinner. Miss Hetherington was. She acknowledged Hilary's bow as the latter passed to her table, but made no attempt to get into conversation with her. On the following day, after making some necessary purchases of clothes and underclothing, Hilary left by train for Fez.

3

It was on the day of Hilary's departure that Mrs.
Calvin Baker coming into the hotel in her usual brisk
fashion, was accosted by Miss Hetherington whose long
thin nose was quivering with excitement.

"I've remembered about the name *Betterton*—the
disappearing scientist. It was in all the papers. About
two months ago."

"Why, now I do remember something. A British
scientist—yes—he'd been at some conference in Paris."

"Yes—that's it. Now I wonder, do you think—this
could possibly be his *wife*? *I* looked in the register and I
see her address is Harwell—Harwell, you know, is the
Atom Station. I do think all these atom bombs are very
wrong. And Cobalt. Such a lovely colour in one's paint-
box and I used it a lot as a child; the worst of all, I
understand *nobody* can survive. We weren't meant to
do these experiments. Somebody told me the other day
that her cousin who is a very shrewd man, said the
whole world might go *radio-active*."

"My my," said Mrs. Calvin Baker.

6

CASABLANCA HAD vaguely disappointed Hilary by being such a prosperous-looking French town with no hint of the Orient or mystery about it, except for the crowds in the streets.

The weather was still perfect, sunny and clear, and she enjoyed looking out of the train at the passing landscape as they journeyed northward. A small Frenchman who looked like a commercial traveller sat opposite to her, in the far corner was a somewhat disapproving-looking nun telling her beads, and two Moorish ladies with a great many packages who conversed gaily with one another, completed the complement of the carriage. Offering a light for her cigarette, the little Frenchman opposite soon entered into conversation. He pointed out things of interest as they passed, and gave her various information about the country. She found him interesting and intelligent.

"You should go to Rabat, Madame. It is a great mistake not to go to Rabat."

"I shall try to do so. But I have not very much time. Besides"—she smiled—"money is short. We can only take so much with us abroad, you know."

"But that is simple. One arranges with a friend here."

"I'm afraid I haven't got a convenient friend in Morocco."

"Next time you travel, Madame, send me a little word. I will give you my card. And I arrange everything. I travel often in England on business and you repay me there. It is all quite simple."

"That's very kind of you, and I hope I shall pay a second visit to Morocco."

"It must be a change for you, Madame, to come here from England. So cold, so foggy, so disagreeable."

"Yes, it's a great change."

"I, too, I travelled from Paris three weeks ago. It was then fog, rain and all of the most disgusting. I arrive here and all is sunshine. Though, mind you, the air is cold. But it is pure. Good pure air. How was the weather in England when you left?"

"Much as you say," said Hilary. "Fog."

"Ah yes, it is the foggy season. Snow—you have had snow this year?"

"No," said Hilary, "there has been no snow." She wondered to herself, amusedly, if this much-travelled little Frenchman was following what he considered to be the correct trend of English conversation, dealing principally with the weather. She asked him a question or two about the political situation in Morocco and in Algiers, and he responded willingly, showing himself to be well informed.

Glancing across at the far corner, Hilary observed the nun's eyes fixed disapprovingly on her. The Moroccan ladies got out and other travellers got in. It was evening when they arrived at Fez.

"Permit me to assist you, Madame."

Hilary was standing, rather bewildered at the bustle and noise of the station. Arab porters were seizing her luggage from her hands, shouting, yelling, calling, recommending different hotels. She turned gratefully to her new French acquaintance.

"You are going to the Palais Jamail, *n'est-ce-pas,* Madame?"

"Yes."

"That is right. It is eight kilometres from here, you understand."

"Eight kilometres?" Hilary was dismayed. "It's not in the town, then."

"It is by the old town," the Frenchman explained. "Me, I stay here at the hotel in the commercial new city. But for the holiday, the rest, the enjoyment, naturally you go to the Palais Jamail. It was a former residence, you understand, of the Moroccan nobility. It has beautiful gardens, and you go straight from it into the old city of Fez which is untouched. It does not seem as though the hotel had sent to meet this train. If you permit, I will arrange for a taxi for you."

"You're very kind, but . . ."

The Frenchman spoke in rapid Arabic to the porters and shortly afterwards Hilary took her place in a taxi, her baggage was pushed in, and the Frenchman told her exactly what to give the rapacious porters. He also dismissed them with a few sharp words of Arabic when they protested that the remuneration was inadequate. He whipped a card from his pocket and handed it to her.

"My car, Madame, and if I can be of assistance to you at any time, tell me. I shall be at the Grand Hotel here for the next four days."

He raised his hat and went away. Hilary looked down at the card which she could just see before they moved out of the lighted station.

Monsieur Henri Laurier

The taxi drove briskly out of the town, through the country, up a hill. Hilary tried to see, looking out of the windows, where she was going, but darkness had set in now. Except when they passed a lighted building nothing much could be seen. Was this perhaps where her

journey diverged from the normal and entered the unknown? Was Monsieur Laurier an emissary from the
organisation that had persuaded Thomas Betterton to
leave his work, his home and his wife? She sat in the
corner of the taxi, nervously apprehensive, wondering
where it was taking her.

It took her, however, in the most exemplary manner
to the Palais Jamail. She dismounted there, passed
through an arched gateway and found herself, with a
thrill of pleasure, in an oriental interior. There were
long divans, coffee tables, and native rugs. From the
reception desk she was taken through several rooms
which led out of each other, out onto a terrace, passing
by orange trees and scented flowers, and then up a
winding staircase and into a pleasant bedroom, still
oriental in style but equipped with all the *conforts
modernes* so necessary to twentieth-century travellers.

Dinner, the porter informed her, took place from
seven-thirty. She unpacked a little, washed, combed her
hair and went downstairs through the long oriental
smoking room, out on the terrace and across and up
some steps to a lighted dining room running at right
angles to it.

The dinner was excellent, and as Hilary ate, various
people came and went from the restaurant. She was
too tired to size them up and classify them this particular evening, but one or two outstanding personalities took her eye. An elderly man, very yellow of face,
with a little goatee beard. She noticed him because of
the extreme deference paid to him by the staff. Plates
were whisked away and placed for him at the mere
raising of his head. The slightest turn of an eyebrow
brought a waiter rushing to his table. She wondered
who he was. The majority of diners were clearly touring
on pleasure trips. There was a German at a big table
in the centre, there was a middle-aged man with a fair,

very beautiful girl who she thought might be Swedes, or possibly Danes. There was an English family with two children, and various groups of travelling Americans. There were three French families.

After dinner she had coffee on the terrace. It was slightly cold but not unduly so and she enjoyed the smell of scented blossoms. She went to bed early.

Sitting on the terrace the following morning in the sunshine under the red striped umbrella that protected her from the sun, Hilary felt how fantastic the whole thing was. Here she sat, pretending to be a dead woman, expecting something melodramatic and out of the common to occur. After all, wasn't it only too likely that poor Olive Betterton had come abroad merely to distract her mind and heart from sad thoughts and feelings? Probably the poor woman had been just as much in the dark as everybody else.

Certainly the words she had said before she died admitted of a perfectly ordinary explanation. She had wanted Thomas Betterton warned against somebody called Boris. Her mind had wandered—she had quoted a strange little jingle—she had gone on to say that she couldn't believe it at first. Couldn't believe what? Possibly only that Thomas Betterton had been spirited away the way he had been.

There had been no sinister undertones, no helpful clues. Hilary stared down at the terrace garden below her. It was beautiful here. Beautiful and peaceful. Children chattered and ran up and down the terrace, French mammas called to them or scolded them. The blonde Swedish girl came and sat down by a table and yawned. She took out a pale pink lipstick and touched up her already exquisitely painted lips. She appraised her face seriously, frowning a little.

Presently her companion—husband, Hilary wondered, or it might possibly be her father—joined her.

She greeted him without a smile. She leaned forward and talked to him, apparently expostulating about something. He protested and apologised.

The old man with the yellow face and the little goatee came up the terrace from the gardens below. He went and sat at a table against the extreme wall, and immediately a waiter darted forth. He gave an order and the waiter bowed before him and went away, in all haste to execute it. The fair girl caught her companion excitedly by the arm and looked towards the elderly man.

Hilary ordered a Martini, and when it came she asked the waiter in a low voice,

"Who is the old man there against the wall?"

"Ah!" The waiter leaned forward dramatically. "That is Monsieur Aristides. He is enormously—but yes, enormously—rich."

He sighed in ecstasy at the contemplation of so much wealth and Hilary looked over at the shrivelled up, bent figure at the far table. Such a wrinkled, dried up, mummified old morsel of humanity. And yet, because of his enormous wealth, waiters darted and sprang and spoke with awe in their voices. Old Monsieur Aristides shifted his position. Just for a moment his eyes met hers. He looked at her for a moment, then looked away.

"Not so insignificant after all," Hilary thought to herself. Those eyes, even at that distance, had been wonderfully intelligent and alive.

The blonde girl and her escort got up from their table and went into the dining room. The waiter who now seemed to consider himself as Hilary's guide and mentor, stopped at her table as he collected glasses and gave her further information.

"*Ce Monsieur là,* he is a big business magnate from Sweden. Very rich, very important. And the lady with

him she is a film star—another Garbo, they say. Very
chic—very beautiful—but does she make him the
scenes, the histories! Nothing pleases her. She is, as
you say, 'fed up' to be here, in Fez, where there are no
jewellers' shops—and no other expensive women to ad-
mire and envy her toilettes. She demands that he should
take her somewhere more amusing tomorrow. Ah, it is
not always the rich who can enjoy the tranquillity and
peace of mind."

Having uttered this last in a somewhat sententious
fashion, he saw a beckoning forefinger and sprang
across the terrace as though galvanised.

"Monsieur?"

Most people had gone in to lunch, but Hilary had
had breakfast late and was in no hurry for her midday
meal. She ordered herself another drink. A good-looking young Frenchman came out of the bar and across
the terrace, cast a swift, discreet glance at Hilary which,
thinly disguised, meant: "Is there anything doing here,
I wonder?" and then went down the steps to the terrace
below. As he did so he half sang, half hummed a snatch
of French opera.

> *"Le long des lauriers roses,*
> *Revant de douces choses."*

The words formed a little pattern on Hilary's brain.
Le long des lauriers roses. Laurier. Laurier? That was
the name of the Frenchman in the train. Was there a
connection here or was it coincidence? She opened her
bag and hunted in it for the card he had given her.
Mons. Henri Laurier, 3 Rue des Croissants, Casablanca.
She turned the card over and there seemed to be faint
pencil marks on the back of it. It was as though something had been written on it and then rubbed out. She
tried to decipher what the marks were. *"Où sont,"* the

message began, then something which she could not decipher, and finally she made out the words *"D'antan."* For a moment she had thought that it might be a message, but now she shook her head and put the card back in her bag. It must have been some quotation that he had written on it and then rubbed out.

A shadow fell on her and she looked up, startled. Mr. Aristides was standing there between her and the sun. His eyes were not on her. He was looking across over the gardens below towards the silhouette of hills in the distance. She heard him sigh and then he turned abruptly towards the dining room and as he did so, the sleeve of his coat caught the glass on her table and sent it flying to the terrace where it broke. He wheeled round quickly and politely.

"Ah. *Mille pardons, Madame."*

Hilary assured him smilingly in French that it did not matter in the least. With the swift flick of a finger he summoned a waiter. The waiter as usual came running. He ordered a replacement of Madame's drink and then once more apologising, he made his way into the restaurant.

The young Frenchman, still humming, came up the steps again. He lingered noticeably as he passed Hilary, but as she gave no sign, he went on into lunch with a slight philosophic shrug of the shoulders.

A French family passed across the terrace, the parents calling to their young.

"Mais viens, donc, Bobo. Qu'est-ce que tu fais? Dépêche-toi!"

"Laisse ta balle, cherie, on va dejeuner."

They passed up the steps and into the restaurant, a happy contented little nucleus of family life. Hilary felt suddenly alone and frightened.

The waiter brought her drink. She asked if M. Aristides was all alone here?

"Oh, Madame, naturally, anyone so rich as M. Aristides would never travel alone. He has here his valet and two secretaries and a chauffeur."

The waiter was quite shocked at the idea of M. Aristides travelling unaccompanied.

Hilary noted, however, when she at last went into the dining room that the old man sat at a table by himself as he had done on the previous evening. At a table nearby sat two young men who she thought were probably the secretaries since she noticed that one or the other of them was always on the alert and looked constantly towards the table where M. Aristides, shrivelled and monkey-like, ate his lunch and did not seem to notice their existence. Evidently to M. Aristides, secretaries were not human!

The afternoon passed in a vague dreamlike manner. Hilary strolled through the gardens, descending from terrace to terrace. The peace and the beauty seemed quite astounding. There was the splash of water, the gleam of the golden oranges, and innumerable scents and fragrances. It was the Oriental atmosphere of seclusion about it that Hilary found so satisfying. *As a garden enclosed is my sister, my spouse* . . . This was what a garden was meant to be, a place shut away from the world—full of green and gold—

If I could stay here, thought Hilary. If I could stay here always . . .

It was not the actual garden of the Palais Jamail that was in her thoughts, it was the state of mind it typified. When she no longer looked for peace, she had found it. And peace of mind had come to her at a moment when she was committed to adventure and danger.

But perhaps there was no danger and no adventure . . . Perhaps she could stay here awhile and nothing would happen . . . and then . . .

And then—what?

A little cold breeze sprang up and Hilary gave a quick shiver. You strayed into the garden of peaceful living, but in the end you would be betrayed from within. The turmoil of the world, the harshness of living, the regrets and despairs, all these she carried within her.

And it was late afternoon, and the sun had lost its power. Hilary went up the various terraces and into the hotel.

In the gloom of the Oriental Lounge, something voluble and cheerful resolved itself, as Hilary's eyes got attuned to the dimness, into Mrs. Calvin Baker, her hair newly blued, and her appearance immaculate as ever.

"I've just got here by air," she explained. "I simply can't stand these trains—the time they take! And the people in them, as often as not, quite unsanitary! They've no idea at all of hygiene in these countries. My dear, you should see the meat in the *souks*—all smothered in flies. They just seem to think it's natural to have flies settling on everything."

"I suppose it is really," said Hilary.

Mrs. Calvin Baker was not going to allow such a heretical statement to pass.

"I'm a great believer in the Clean Food movement. At home everything perishable is wrapped in cellophane—but even in London your bread and cakes just stand about unwrapped. Now tell me, have you been getting around? You've been doing the old city today, I expect?"

"I'm afraid I haven't 'done' anything," said Hilary, smiling. "I've just been sitting about in the sun."

"Ah, of course—you're just out of hospital. I forgot." Clearly only recent illness was accepted by Mrs. Calvin Baker as an excuse for failure to sight-see. "How could I be so stupid? Why, it's perfectly true, after concussion you ought to lie down and rest in a dark room most of the day. By and by we can make some expeditions together. I'm one of those people who like a real packed day—everything planned and arranged. Every minute filled."

In Hilary's present mood, this sounded like a foretaste of hell, but she congratulated Mrs. Calvin Baker on her energy.

"Well, I will say that for a woman of my age I get around pretty well. I hardly ever feel fatigue. Do you remember Miss Hetherington at Casablanca? An Englishwoman with a long face. She'll be arriving this evening. She prefers train to flying. Who's staying in the hotel? Mostly French, I suppose. And honeymoon couples. I must run along now and see about my room. I didn't like the one they gave me and they promised to change it."

A miniature whirlwind of energy, Mrs. Calvin Baker departed.

When Hilary entered the dining room that evening, the first thing she saw was Miss Hetherington at a small table against the wall eating her dinner with a Penguin book propped up in front of her.

The three ladies had coffee together after dinner and Miss Hetherington displayed a pleasurable excitement over the Swedish magnate and the blonde film star.

"Not married, I understand," she breathed, disguising her pleasure with a correct disapproval. "One sees so much of that sort of thing abroad. That seemed a nice French family at the table by the window. The children seemed so fond of their papa. Of course, French children are allowed to sit up far too late. Ten o'clock sometimes before they go to bed, and they go through every course of the menu instead of just having milk and biscuits as children should."

"They seem to look quite healthy on it," said Hilary laughing.

Miss Hetherington shook her head and uttered a cluck of disapproval.

"They'll pay for it later," she said with grim foreboding. "Their parents even let them drink *wine*."

Horror could go no further.

Mrs. Calvin Baker began making plans for the next day.

"I don't think I shall go to the old city," she said. "I did that very thoroughly last time. Most interesting and quite a labyrinth, if you know what I mean. So quaint and old world. If I hadn't had the guide with me, I don't think I should have found my way back to the hotel. You just kind of lose your sense of direction. But the guide was a very nice man and told me quite a lot of interesting things. He has a brother in the States—in Chicago, I think he said. Then when we'd finished with the town, he took me up to a kind of eating house or tea room, right up on the hillsides looking down over the old city—a marvellous view. I had to drink that dreadful mint tea, of course, which is really very nasty. And they wanted me to buy various things, some quite nice, but some just rubbish. One has to be very firm, I find."

"Yes, indeed," said Miss Hetherington.

She added rather wistfully, "And, of course, one can't really spare the money for souvenirs. These money restrictions are so worrying."

7

HILARY HOPED TO AVOID having to see the old city of
Fez in the depressing company of Miss Hetherington.
Fortunately the latter was invited by Mrs. Baker to
come with her on an expedition by car. Since Mrs.
Baker made it clear that she was going to pay for the
car, Miss Hetherington, whose travelling allowance was
dwindling in an alarming manner, accepted with avid-
ity. Hilary, after inquiry at the desk, was supplied with
a guide, and set forth to see the city of Fez.

They started from the terrace, going down through
the succession of terraced gardens until they reached
an enormous door in the wall at the bottom. The guide
produced a key of mammoth proportions, unlocked the
door which swung slowly open, and motioned Hilary to
pass through.

It was like stepping into another world. All about her
were the walls of Old Fez. Narrow winding streets, high
walls, and occasionally, through a doorway, a glimpse
of an interior or a courtyard, and moving all around
her were laden donkeys, men with their burdens, boys,
women veiled and unveiled, the whole busy secret life
of this Moorish city. Wandering through the narrow
streets she forgot everything else, her mission, the past
tragedy of her life, even herself. She was all eyes and
ears, living and walking in a dream world. The only
annoyance was the guide who talked unceasingly, and
urged her into various establishments into which she
had no particular wish to go.

"You look, lady. This man have very nice things, very cheap, really old, really Moorish. He have gowns and silks. You like very nice beads?"

The eternal commerce of East selling to West went on, but it hardly disturbed the charm for Hilary. She soon lost all sense of place or direction. Here within this walled city she had little idea of whether she was walking north or south or whether she was retracing her steps over the same streets through which she had already passed. She was quite exhausted when the guide made his final suggestion, which was evidently part of the routine.

"I take you very nice house, now, very superior. Friends of mine. You have mint tea there and they show you plenty lovely things."

Hilary recognised the well-known gambit which Mrs. Calvin Baker had described. However, she was willing to see, or be taken to see, anything that was suggested. Tomorrow, she promised herself, she would come into the Old City alone and wander around without a guide chattering by her elbow. So she allowed herself to be guided through a gateway and up a winding path climbing up more or less outside the city walls. They arrived at last at a garden surrounding an attractive house built in native style.

Here in a big room with a fine view out over the city, she was urged to sit down at a small coffee table. In due course glasses of mint tea were brought. To Hilary who did not like sugar with her tea, it was somewhat of an ordeal to drink it. But by banishing the idea of tea from her mind, and merely thinking of it as a new kind of lemonade, she managed almost to enjoy it. She enjoyed, too, being shown rugs and beads and draperies, embroideries and various other things. She made one or two small purchases more out of good manners than for any other reason. The indefatigable guide then said,

"I have car ready now and take you very nice short drive. One hour, not more, see very beautiful scenery and country. And then back to hotel." He added, assuming a suitably discreet expression, "This girl here, she take you first to very nice ladies' toilet."

The girl who had served the tea was standing by them smiling, and said at once in careful English,

"Yes, yes, Madame. You come with me. We have very fine toilet, oh very fine. Just like the Ritz Hotel. Same as in New York or Chicago. You see!"

Smiling a little, Hilary followed the girl. The toilet hardly rose to the heights claimed for it, but it did at least have running water. There was a wash basin and a small cracked mirror which had such distorting proportions that Hilary almost shrank back in alarm at the sight of her own face. When she had washed and dried her hands, which she did on her own handkerchief, not much caring for the appearance of the towel, she turned to leave.

In some way, however, the door of the toilet appeared to have stuck. She turned and rattled the handle unavailingly. It would not move. Hilary wondered whether it had been bolted or locked from the outside. She grew angry. What was the idea of shutting her in there? Then she noticed that there was another door in a corner of the room. Going to it she turned the handle. This time the door opened easily enough. She passed through.

She found herself in a small eastern looking room with light that came only from slits high in the wall. Sitting there on a low divan, smoking, was the little Frenchman she had met in the train, M. Henri Laurier.

2

He did not rise to greet her. He merely said, and the timbre of his voice was slightly changed,

"Good afternoon, Mrs. Betterton."

For a moment Hilary stood motionless. Astonishment held her in its grip. So this—was *it!* She pulled herself together. "This is what you've been expecting. Act as you think *she* would act." She came forward and said eagerly,

"You have news for me? You can help me?"

He nodded, then said reproachfully:

"I found you, Madame, somewhat obtuse upon the train. Perhaps you are too well accustomed to talk of the weather."

"The weather?" she stared at him, bewildered.

What had he said about the weather on the train? Cold? Fog? Snow?

Snow. That was what Olive Betterton had whispered as she lay dying. And she had quoted a silly little jingle —what was it?

> *Snow, snow, beautiful snow,*
> *You slip on a lump and over you go.*

Hilary repeated it falteringly now.

"Exactly—why did you not respond with that immediately as ordered?"

"You don't understand. I have been ill. I was in a plane crash and afterwards in hospital with concussion. It's affected my memory in all sorts of ways. Everything long ago is clear enough, but there are terrible blanks—great gaps." She let her hands rise to her head. She found it easy enough to go on with a real tremor in her voice. "You can't understand how frightening that is. I keep feeling that I've forgotten important things—really important things. The more I try to get them back, the less they will come."

"Yes," said Laurier, "the aeroplane crash was unfortunate." He spoke in a cold businesslike way. "It is going to be a question of whether you have the necessary stamina and courage to continue your journey."

"Of course I'm going to continue my journey," cried Hilary. "My husband—" her voice broke.

He smiled, but not a very pleasant smile. Faintly cat-like.

"Your husband," he said, "is I understand, awaiting you with eagerness."

Hilary's voice broke.

"You have no idea," she said, "no idea of what it's been like these months since he went away."

"Do you think the British authorities came to a definite conclusion as to what you did or did not know?"

Hilary stretched out her hands with a wide gesture.

"How do I know—how can I tell? They *seemed* satisfied."

"All the same . . ." he stopped.

"I think it quite possible," said Hilary slowly, "that I have been followed here. I can't pick out any one particular person but I have had the feeling ever since I left England that I am under observation."

"Naturally," said Laurier, coldly. "We expected no less."

"I thought I ought to warn you."

"My dear Mrs. Betterton, we are not children. We understand what we are doing."

"I'm sorry," said Hilary, humbly. "I'm afraid I'm very ignorant."

"It does not matter if you are ignorant so long as you are obedient."

"I shall be obedient," said Hilary in a low voice.

"You were closely watched in England, I have no doubt, ever since the day of your husband's departure. Nevertheless, the message came to you, did it not?"

"Yes," said Hilary.

"Now," said Laurier in a businesslike manner, "I will give you your instructions, Madame."

"Please do."

"From here you will proceed to Marrakesh the day after tomorrow. That is as you planned and in accordance with your reservations."

"Yes."

"The day after you arrive there you will receive a telegram from England. What it will say I do not know, but it will be sufficient for you to make plans immediately to return to England."

"I am to *return to England?*"

"Please listen. I have not finished. You will book a seat on a plane leaving Casablanca the following day."

"Supposing I cannot get reservations—supposing the seats are all booked?"

"They will not be all booked. Everything is arranged for. Now, you understand your instructions?"

"I understand."

"Then please return to where your guide is waiting. You have been long enough in this ladies' toilet. By the way, you have become friendly with an American woman and an English woman who are now staying at the Palais Jamail?"

"Yes. Has that been a mistake? It has been difficult to avoid."

"Not at all. It suits our plans admirably. If you can persuade one or other of them to accompany you to Marrakesh, so much the better. Goodbye, Madame."

"Au revoir, Monsieur."

"It is unlikely," Monsieur Laurier told her with a complete lack of interest, "that I shall meet you again."

Hilary retraced her steps to the ladies' toilet. This time she found the other door unfastened. A few minutes later she had rejoined the guide in the tea room.

"I got very nice car waiting," said the guide. "I take you now for very pleasant instructive drive."

The expedition proceeded according to plan.

3

"So you're leaving for Marrakesh tomorrow," said Miss Hetherington. "You haven't made a very long stay in Fez, have you? Wouldn't it have been much easier to go to Marrakesh first and then to Fez, returning to Casablanca afterwards?"

"I suppose it would really," said Hilary, "but reservations are rather difficult to obtain. It's pretty crowded here."

"Not with English people," said Miss Hetherington, rather disconsolately. "It really seems dreadful nowadays the way one meets hardly *any* of one's fellow countrymen." She looked round her disparagingly and said, "It's all the French."

Hilary smiled faintly. The fact that Morocco was a French colonial possession did not seem to count much with Miss Hetherington. Hotels anywhere abroad she regarded as the prerogative of the English travelling public.

"The French and the Germans *and* the Greeks," said Mrs. Calvin Baker, with a little cackle of laughter. "That scruffy little old man is a Greek, I believe."

"I was told he was Greek," said Hilary.

"Looks like a person of importance," said Mrs. Baker. "You see how the waiters fly about him."

"They give the English hardly any attention nowadays," said Miss Hetherington, gloomily. "They always give them the most terrible back bedrooms—the ones maids and valets used to have in the old days."

"Well, I can't say I've found any fault with the accommodation I've had since I came to Morocco," said Mrs. Calvin Baker. "I've managed to get a most comfortable room and bath every time."

"You're an American," said Miss Hetherington, sharply, and with some venom in her voice. She clicked her knitting needles furiously.

"I wish I could persuade you two to come to Marrakesh with me," said Hilary. "It's been so pleasant meeting you and talking to you here. Really, it's very lonely travelling all by oneself."

"I've *been* to Marrakesh," said Miss Hetherington in a shocked voice.

Mrs. Calvin Baker, however, appeared to be somewhat sold on the idea.

"Well, it certainly is an idea," she said. "It's over a month since I was in Marrakesh. I'd be glad to go there again for a spell, and I could show you around, too, Mrs. Betterton and prevent you being imposed upon. It's not until you've been to a place and looked around it that you learn the ropes. I wonder now. I'll go to the office and see what I can fix up."

Miss Hetherington said acidly, when she had departed,

"That's exactly like these American women. Rushing from place to place, never settling down anywhere. Egypt one day, Palestine the next. Sometimes I really don't think they know what country they're in."

She shut her lips with a snap and rising and gathering up her knitting carefully, she left the Turkish room with a little nod to Hilary as she went. Hilary glanced down at her watch. She felt inclined not to change this evening for dinner, as she usually did. She sat on there alone in the low, rather dark room with its Oriental hangings. A waiter looked in, then went away after turning on two lamps. They did not give out very much light and the room seemed pleasantly dim. It had an Eastern sort of serenity. Hilary sat back on the low divan, thinking of the future.

Only yesterday she had been wondering if the whole business upon which she had been engaged was a mare's nest. And now—now she was on the point of starting on her real journey. She must be careful, very careful. She must make no slip. She must be Olive Betterton, moderately well educated, inartistic, conventional but with definite Left Wing sympathies, and a woman who was devoted to her husband.

"I must make no mistake," said Hilary to herself, under her breath.

How strange it felt to be sitting here alone in Morocco. She felt as though she had got into a land of mystery and enchantment. That dim lamp beside her! If she were to take the carved brass between her hands and rub, would a Djin of the Lamp appear? As the thought came to her, she started. Materialising quite suddenly from beyond the lamp, she saw the small wrinkled face and pointed beard of Mr. Aristides. He bowed politely before sitting down beside her, saying,

"You permit, Madame?"

Hilary responded politely.

Taking out his cigarette case he offered her a cigarette. She accepted and he lit one himself also.

"It pleases you, this country, Madame?" he asked after a moment or two.

"I have been here only a very short time," said Hilary. "I find it so far quite enchanting."

"Ah. And you have been into the old city? You liked it?"

"I think it is wonderful."

"Yes, it is wonderful. It is the past there—the past of commerce, of intrigue, of whispering voices, shuttered activities, all the mystery and passion of a city enclosed in its narrow streets and walls. Do you know what I think of, Madame, when I walk through the streets of Fez?"

"No?"

"I think of your Great West Road in London. I think of your great factory buildings on each side of the road. I think of those buildings lit throughout with their neon lighting and the people inside, that you see so clearly from the road as you drive along in your car. There is nothing hidden, there is nothing mysterious. There are not even curtains to the windows. No, they do their work there with the whole world observing them if it wants to do so. It is like slicing off the top of an ant-hill."

"You mean," said Hilary, interested, "that it is the contrast that interests you?"

Mr. Aristides nodded his elderly, tortoiselike head.

"Yes," he said. "There everything is in the open and in the old streets of Fez nothing is *à jour*. Everything is hidden, dark. . . . *But*—" he leant forward and tapped a finger on the little brass coffee table "—but the same things go on. The same cruelties, the same oppression, the same wish for power, the same bargaining and haggling."

"You think that human nature is the same everywhere?" Hilary asked.

"In every country. In the past as in the present there are always the two things that rule. Cruelty and benevolence! One or the other. Sometimes both." He continued with hardly a change of manner, "They have told me, Madame, that you were in a very bad aeroplane accident the other day at Casablanca?"

"Yes, that is true."

"I envy you," Mr. Aristides said unexpectedly.

Hilary looked at him in an astonished manner. Again he waggled his head in vehement assertion.

"Yes," he added, "you are to be envied. You have had an experience. I should like the experience of having come so near to death. To have that, yet survive —do you not feel yourself different since then, Madame?"

"In a rather unfortunate way," said Hilary. "I had concussion and that gives me very bad headaches, and it also affects my memory."

"Those are mere inconveniences," said Mr. Aristides with a wave of the hand, "but it is an adventure of the spirit you have passed through, is it not?"

"It is true," said Hilary slowly, "that I have passed through an adventure of the spirit."

She was thinking of a bottle of Vichy water and a little heap of sleeping pills.

"I have never had that experience," said Mr. Aristides in his dissatisfied voice. "So many other things, but not that."

He rose, bowed, said, *"Mes hommages, Madame,"* and left her.

8

How ALIKE, Hilary thought to herself, all airports were!
They had a strange anonymity about them. They were
all at some distance from the town or city they served,
and in consequence you had a queer, stateless feeling of
existing nowhere. You could fly from London to Ma-
drid, to Rome, to Istanbul, to Cairo, to anywhere you
liked and if your journey was a through one by air, you
would never have the faintest idea of what any of these
cities looked like! If you caught a glimpse of them from
the air, they were only a kind of glorified map, something built with a child's box of bricks.

And why, she thought vexedly, looking round her,
does one always have to be at these places so much too
early?

They had spent nearly half an hour in the waiting
room. Mrs. Calvin Baker, who had decided to accompany Hilary to Marrakesh had been talking non-stop
ever since their arrival. Hilary had answered almost
mechanically. But now she realised that the flow had
been diverted. Mrs. Baker had now switched her attention to two other travellers who were sitting near her.
They were both tall, fair young men. One an American
with a broad, friendly grin, the other a rather solemn
looking Dane or Norwegian. The Dane talked heavily,
slowly, and rather pedantically in careful English. The
American was clearly delighted to find another American traveller. Presently, in conscientious fashion, Mrs.
Calvin Baker turned to Hilary.

"Mr—? I'd like to have you know my friend, Mrs. Betterton."

"Andrew Peters—Andy to my friends."

The other young man rose to his feet, bowed rather stiffly and said, "Torquil Ericsson."

"So now we're all acquainted," said Mrs. Baker happily. "Are we all going to Marrakesh? It's my friend's first visit there—"

"I, too," said Ericsson. "I, too, for the first time go."

"That goes for me too," said Peters.

The loud speaker was suddenly switched on and a hoarse announcement in French was made. The words were barely distinguishable but it appeared to be their summons to the plane.

There were four passengers besides Mrs. Baker and Hilary. Besides Peters and Ericsson, there was a thin, tall Frenchman, and a severe-looking nun.

It was a clear, sunny day and flying conditions were good. Leaning back in her seat with half closed eyes, Hilary studied her fellow passengers, seeking to distract herself that way from the anxious questionings which were going on in her mind.

One seat ahead of her, on the other side of the aisle, Mrs. Calvin Baker in her grey travelling costume looked like a plump and contented duck. A small hat with wings was perched on her blue hair and she was turning the pages of a glossy magazine. Occasionally she leaned forward to tap the shoulder of the man sitting in front of her, who was the cheerful-looking fair young American, Peters. When she did so he turned round, displaying his good-humored grin, and responding energetically to her remarks. How very good natured and friendly Americans were, Hilary thought to herself. So different from the stiff travelling English. She could not imagine Miss Hetherington, for instance, falling into easy conversation with a young man even of her own

nation, on a plane, and she doubted if the latter would
have responded as good-naturedly as this young American was doing.

Across the aisle from her was the Norwegian, Ericsson.

As she caught his eye, he made her a stiff little bow
and leaning across offered her his magazine, which he
was just closing. She thanked him and took it. In the
seat behind him was the thin, dark Frenchman. His legs
were stretched out and he seemed to be asleep.

Hilary turned her head over her shoulder. The
severe-faced nun was sitting behind her, and the nun's
eyes, impersonal, incurious, met Hilary's with no expression in them. She sat immovable, her hands clasped.
It seemed to Hilary an odd trick of Time that a woman
in traditional mediaeval costume should be travelling by
air in the twentieth century.

Six people, thought Hilary, travelling together for a
few hours, travelling to different places with different
aims, scattering perhaps at the end of that few hours
and never meeting again. She had read a novel which
had hinged on a similar theme and where the lives of
those six people were followed up. The Frenchman, she
thought, must be on a holiday. He seemed so tired. The
young American was perhaps a student of some kind.
Ericsson was perhaps going to take a job. The nun was
doubtless bound for her convent.

Hilary closed her eyes and forgot her fellow travellers. She puzzled, as she had done all last night, over the
instructions that had been given her. She was to return
to England! It seemed crazy! Or could it be that in
some way she had been found wanting, was not trusted:
had failed to supply certain words or credentials that
the real Olive would have supplied. She sighed and
moved restlessly. "Well," she thought, "I can do no

more than I am doing. If I've failed—I've failed. At any rate, I've done my best."

Then another thought struck her. Henri Laurier had accepted it as natural and inevitable that a close watch was being kept upon her in Morocco—was this a means of disarming suspicion? With the abrupt return of Mrs. Betterton to England it would surely be assumed that she had *not* come to Morocco in order to "disappear" like her husband. Suspicion would relax—she would be regarded as a *bona fide* traveller.

She would leave for England, going by Air France via Paris—and perhaps in Paris—

Yes, of course—in Paris. In Paris where Tom Betterton had disappeared. How much easier to stage a disappearance there. Perhaps Tom Betterton had never left Paris. Perhaps—tired of profitless speculation Hilary went to sleep. She woke—dozed again, occasionally glancing, without interest, at the magazine she held. Awakening suddenly from a deeper sleep, she noticed that the plane was rapidly losing height and circling round. She glanced at her watch, but it was still some time earlier than the estimated time of arrival. Moreover, looking down through the window, she could not see any signs of an aerodrome beneath.

For a moment a faint qualm of apprehension struck her. The thin dark Frenchman rose, yawned, stretched his arms and looked out and said something in French which she did not catch. But Ericsson leant across the aisle and said,

"We are coming down here, it seems—but why?"

Mrs. Calvin Baker, leaning out of her seat, turned her head and nodded brightly as Hilary said,

"We seem to be landing."

The plane swooped round in ever lower circles. The country beneath them seemed to be practically desert. There were no signs of houses or villages. The wheels

touched with a decided bump, bouncing along and taxi-
ing until they finally stopped. It had been a somewhat
rough landing, but it was a landing in the middle of
nowhere.

Had something gone wrong with the engine, Hilary
wondered, or had they run out of petrol? The pilot, a
dark-skinned, handsome young man, came through the
forward door and along the plane.

"If you please," he said, "you will all get out."

He opened the rear door, let down a short ladder
and stood there waiting for them all to pass out. They
stood in a little group on the ground, shivering a little.
It was chilly here, with the wind blowing sharply from
the mountains in the distance. The mountains, Hilary
noticed, were covered with snow and singularly beautiful. The air was crisply cold and intoxicating. The pilot
descended too, and addressed them, speaking French:

"You are all here? Yes? Excuse, please, you will have
to wait a little minute, perhaps. Ah, no, I see it is
arriving."

He pointed to where a small dot on the horizon was
gradually growing nearer. Hilary said in a slightly bewildered voice:

"But why have we come down here? What is the
matter? How long shall we have to be here?"

The French traveller said,

"There is, I understand, a station wagon arriving. We
shall go on in that."

"Did the engine fail?" asked Hilary.

Andy Peters smiled cheerfully.

"Why no, I shouldn't say so," he said, "the engine
sounded all right to me. However, they'll fix up something of that kind, no doubt."

She stared, puzzled. Mrs. Calvin Baker murmured,

"My, but it's chilly, standing about here. That's the

worst of this climate. It seems so sunny but it's cold the moment you get near sunset."

The pilot was murmuring under his breath, swearing, Hilary thought. He was saying something like:

"Toujours des retards insupportables."

The station wagon came towards them at a breakneck pace. The Berber driver drew up with a grinding of brakes. He sprang down and was immediately engaged by the pilot in angry conversation. Rather to Hilary's surprise, Mrs. Baker intervened in the dispute —speaking in French.

"Don't waste time," she said peremptorily. "What's the good of arguing? We want to get out of here."

The driver shrugged his shoulders, and going to the station wagon, he unhitched the back part of it which let down. Inside was a large packing case. Together with the pilot and with help from Ericsson and Peters, they got it down on to the ground. From the effort it took, it seemed to be heavy. Mrs. Calvin Baker put her hand on Hilary's arm and said, as the man began to raise the lid of the case,

"I shouldn't watch, my dear. It's never a pretty sight."

She led Hilary a little way away, on the other side of the wagon. The Frenchman and Peters came with them. The Frenchman said in his own language,

"What is it then, this manoeuvre there that they do?"

Mrs. Baker said,

"You are Dr. Barron?"

The Frenchman bowed.

"Pleased to meet you," said Mrs. Baker. She stretched out her hand, rather like a hostess welcoming him to a party. Hilary said in a bewildered tone,

"But I don't understand. What is in that case? Why is it better not to look?"

Andy Peters looked down on her consideringly. He

had a nice face, Hilary thought. Something square and dependable about it. He said,

"I know what it is. The pilot told me. It's not very pretty perhaps, but I guess it's necessary." He added quietly, "There are bodies in there."

"Bodies!" She stared at him.

"Oh, they haven't been murdered or anything," he grinned reassuringly. "They were obtained in a perfectly legitimate way for research—medical research, you know."

But Hilary still stared.

"I don't understand."

"Ah. You see, Mrs. Betterton, this is where the journey ends. One journey, that is."

"Ends?"

"Yes. They'll arrange the bodies in that plane and then the pilot will fix things and presently, as we're driving away from here, we shall see in the distance the flames going up in the air. Another plane that has crashed and come down in flames, *and no survivors!*"

"But why? How fantastic!"

"But surely—" It was Dr. Barron now who spoke to her. "But surely you know where we are going?"

Mrs. Baker, drawing near, said cheerfully,

"Of course she knows. But maybe she didn't expect it quite so soon."

Hilary said, after a short bewildered pause,

"But you mean—all of us?" She looked round.

"We're fellow travellers," said Peters gently.

The young Norwegian, nodding his head, said with an almost fanatical enthusiasm,

"Yes, we are all fellow travellers."

9

THE PILOT came up to them.

"You will start now, please," he said. "As soon as possible. There is much to be done, and we are late on schedule."

Hilary recoiled for a moment. She put her hand nervously to her throat. The pearl choker she was wearing broke under the strain of her fingers. She picked up the loose pearls and crammed them into her pocket.

They all got into the station wagon. Hilary was on a long bench crowded up with Peters one side of her and Mrs. Baker the other. Turning her head towards the American woman, Hilary said,

"So you—so you—are what you might call the liaison officer, Mrs. Baker?"

"That hits it off exactly. And though I say it myself, I'm well qualified. Nobody is surprised to find an American woman getting around and travelling a lot."

She was still plump and smiling, but Hilary sensed, or thought she sensed, a difference. The slight fatuity and surface conventionality had gone. This was an efficient, probably ruthless woman.

"It will make a fine sensation in the headlines," said Mrs. Baker. She laughed with some enjoyment. *"You,* I mean, my dear. Persistently dogged by ill-luck, they'll say. First nearly losing your life in the crash at Casablanca, then being killed in this further disaster."

Hilary realised suddenly the cleverness of the plan.

101

"These others?" she murmured. "Are they who they say they are?"

"Why yes. Dr. Barron is a bacteriologist, I believe. Mr. Ericsson a very brilliant young physicist, Mr. Peters is a research chemist, Miss Needheim, of course, isn't a nun, she's an endocrinologist. Me, as I say, I'm only the liaison officer. I don't belong in this scientific bunch." She laughed again as she said, "That Hetherington woman never had a chance."

"Miss Hetherington—was she—was she—"

Mrs. Baker nodded emphatically.

"If you ask me, she's been tailing you. Took over in Casablanca from whoever followed you out."

"But she didn't come with us today although I urged her to?"

"That wouldn't have been in character," said Mrs. Baker. "It would have looked a little too obvious to go back again to Marrakesh after having been there already. No, she'll have sent a telegram or a phone message through and there'll be someone waiting at Marrakesh to pick you up when you arrive. When you arrive! That's a good laugh, isn't it? Look! Look there now! Up she goes."

They had been driving rapidly away across the desert, and now as Hilary craned forward to look through the little window, she saw a great glow behind them. A faint sound of an explosion came to her ears. Peters threw his head back and laughed. He said:

"Six people die when plane to Marrakesh crashes!"

Hilary said almost under her breath:

"It's—it's rather frightening."

"Stepping off into the unknown?" It was Peters who spoke. He was serious enough now. "Yes, but it's the only way. We're leaving the Past and stepping out towards the Future." His face lit up with sudden enthusiasm. "We've got to get quit of all the bad, mad old stuff. Corrupt governments and the warmongers. We've got to go into the new world—the world of science, clean away from the scum and the driftwood."

Hilary drew a deep breath.

"That's like the things my husband used to say," she said, deliberately.

"Your husband?" He shot her a quick glance. "Why, was he *Tom* Betterton?"

Hilary nodded.

"Well that's great. I never knew him out in the States, though I nearly met him more than once. ZE Fission is one of the most brilliant discoveries of this age—yes, I certainly take my hat off to him. Worked with old Mannheim, didn't he?"

"Yes," said Hilary.

"Didn't they tell me he'd married Mannheim's daughter? But surely *you're* not—"

"I'm his second wife," said Hilary, flushing a little. "He—his—Elsa died in America."

"I remember. Then he went to Britain to work there. Then he riled them by disappearing." He laughed suddenly. "Walked slap out of some Paris Conference into nowhere." He added, as though in further appreciation, "Lord, you can't say they don't organise well."

Hilary agreed with him. The excellence of their organisation was sending a cold pang of apprehension through her. All the plans, codes, signs that had been so elaborately arranged were going to be useless now, for now there would be no trail to pick up. Things had been so arranged that everyone on the fatal plane had been fellow travellers bound for the Unknown Destination where Thomas Betterton had gone before them. There would be no trace left. Nothing. Nothing but a burnt-out plane. Could they—was it possible that Jessop and his organisation could guess that she, Hilary, was *not* one of those charred bodies? She doubted it.

The accident had been so convincing, so clever—there would even be charred bodies in the plane.

Peters spoke again. His voice was boyish with enthusiasm. For him there were no qualms, no looking back, only eagerness to go forward.

"I wonder," he said, "where do we go from here?"

Hilary, too, wondered, because again much depended on that. Sooner or later there must be contacts with humanity. Sooner or later, if investigation was made, the fact that a station wagon with six people in it resembling the description of those who had left that morning by plane, might possibly be noted by someone. She turned to Mrs. Baker, and asked, trying to make her tone the counterpart of the childish eagerness of the young American beside her,

"Where are we going—what happens next?"

"You'll see," said Mrs. Baker, and for all the pleasantness of her voice, there was something somehow ominous in those words.

They drove on. Behind them the flare of the plane still showed in the sky, showed all the more clearly because the sun was now directly below the horizon. Night fell. Still they drove. The going was bad since they were obviously not on any main road. Sometimes they seemed to be on field tracks, at other times they drove over open country.

For a long time Hilary remained awake, thoughts and apprehensions turning round in her head excitedly. But at last, shaken and tossed from side to side, exhaustion had its way and she fell asleep. It was a broken sleep. Various ruts and jars in the road awoke her. For a moment or two she would wonder confusedly where she was, then reality would come back to her. She would remain awake for a few moments, her thoughts racing round in confused apprehension, then once more her head would drop forward and nod, and once again she would sleep.

She was awakened suddenly by the car coming to an abrupt stop. Very gently Peters shook her by the arm.

"Wake up," he said, "we seem to have arrived somewhere."

Everyone got out of the station wagon. They were all cramped and weary. It was still dark and they seemed to have drawn up outside a house surrounded by palm trees. Some distance away they could see a few dim lights as though there were a village there. Guided by a lantern they were ushered into the house. It was a native house with a couple of giggling Berber women who stared curiously at Hilary and Mrs. Calvin Baker. They took no interest in the nun.

The three women were taken to a small upstairs room. There were three mattresses on the floor and some heaps of coverings, but no other furniture.

"I'll say I'm stiff," said Mrs. Baker. "Gets you kind of cramped, riding along the way we've been doing."

"Discomfort does not matter," said the nun.

She spoke with a harsh, guttural assurance. Her English, Hilary found, was good and fluent, though her accent was bad.

"You're living up to your part, Miss Needheim," said the American woman. "I can just see you in the convent, kneeling on the hard stones at four in the morning."

Miss Needheim smiled contemptuously.

"Christianity has made fools of women," she said. "Such a worship of weakness, such snivelling humiliation! Pagan women had strength. They rejoiced and conquered! And in order to conquer, no discomfort is unbearable. Nothing is too much to suffer."

"Right now," said Mrs. Baker, yawning, "I wish I was in my bed at the Palais Jamail at Fez. What about you, Mrs. Betterton? That shaking hasn't done your concussion any good, I'll bet."

"No, it hasn't," Hilary said.

"They'll bring us something to eat presently, and then I'll fix you up with some aspirin and you'd better get to sleep as fast as you can."

Steps were heard coming up the stairs outside and giggling female voices. Presently the two Berber women came into the room. They carried a tray with a big dish of semolina and meat stew. They put it down on the floor, came back again with a metal basin with water in it and a towel. One of them felt Hilary's coat, passing the stuff between her fingers and speaking to the other woman who nodded her head in rapid agreement, and did the same to Mrs. Baker. Neither of them paid any attention to the nun.

"Shoo," said Mrs. Baker, waving them away. "Shoo, shoo."

It was exactly like shooing chickens. The women retreated, still laughing, and left the room.

"Silly creatures," said Mrs. Baker, "it's hard to have patience with them. I suppose babies and clothes are their only interest in life."

"It is all they are fit for," said Fraulein Needheim, "they belong to a slave race. They are useful to serve their betters, but no more."

"Aren't you a little harsh?" said Hilary, irritated by the woman's attitude.

"I have no patience with sentimentality. There are those that rule, the few; and there are the many that serve."

"But surely . . ."

Mrs. Baker broke in in an authoritative manner.

"We've all got our own ideas on these subjects, I

guess," she said, "and very interesting they are. But this is hardly the time for them. We'll want to get what rest we can."

Mint tea arrived. Hilary swallowed some aspirin willingly enough, since her headache was quite a genuine one. Then the three women lay down on the mattresses and fell asleep.

They slept late into the following day. They were not to go on again until the evening, so Mrs. Baker informed them. From the room in which they had slept, there was an outside staircase leading onto a flat roof where they had a certain amount of view over the surrounding country. A little distance away was a village, but here where they were, the house was isolated in a large palm garden. On awakening, Mrs. Baker had indicated three heaps of clothing which had been brought and laid down just inside the door.

"We're going native for the next lap," she explained, "we leave our other clothes here."

So the smart little American woman's neat suiting and Hilary's tweed coat and skirt and the nun's habit were all laid aside and three native Moroccan women sat on the roof of the house and chatted together. The whole thing had a curiously unreal feeling.

Hilary studied Miss Needheim more closely now that she had left the anonymity of her nun's habit. She was a younger woman than Hilary had thought her, not more, perhaps, than thirty-three or thirty-four. There was a neat spruceness in her appearance. The pale skin, the short stubby fingers, and the cold eyes in which burned from time to time the gleam of the fanatic, repelled rather than attracted. Her speech was brusque and uncompromising. Towards both Mrs. Baker and Hilary she displayed a certain amount of contempt as towards people unworthy to associate with her. This arrogance Hilary found very irritating. Mrs. Baker, on the other hand, seemed hardly to notice it. In a queer way Hilary felt nearer and more in sympathy with the two giggling Berber women who brought them food, than with her two companions of the Western world. The young German woman was obviously indifferent to the impression she created. There was a certain concealed impatience in her manner, and it was obvious that she was longing to get on with her journey and that she had no interest in her two companions.

Appraising Mrs. Baker's attitude, Hilary found more difficult. At first Mrs. Baker seemed a natural and normal person after the inhumanity of the German woman specialist. But as the sun sank lower in the sky she felt almost more intrigued and repelled by Mrs. Baker than by Helga Needheim. Mrs. Baker's social manner was almost robotlike in its perfection. All her comments and remarks were natural, normal, everyday currency, but one had a suspicion that the whole thing was like an actor playing a part for perhaps the seven hundredth time. It was an automatic performance, completely divorced from what Mrs. Baker might really have been thinking or feeling. Who was Mrs. Calvin Baker, Hilary wondered? Why had she come to play her part with such machinelike perfection? Was she, too, a fanatic? Had she dreams of a brave new world—was she in violent revolt against the capitalist system? Had she given up all normal life because of her political beliefs and aspirations? Impossible to tell.

They resumed their journey that evening. It was no longer the station wagon. This time it was an open touring car. Everyone was in native dress, the men with white jellabas round them, the women with their faces hidden. Packed tightly in, they started off once more, driving all through the night.

"How are you feeling, Mrs. Betterton?"

Hilary smiled up at Andy Peters. The sun had just

risen and they had stopped for breakfast. Native bread, eggs, and tea made over a primus.

"I feel as though I were taking part in a dream," said Hilary.

"Yes, it has rather that quality."

"Where are we?"

He shrugged his shoulders.

"Who knows? Our Mrs. Calvin Baker, no doubt, but no other."

"It's a very lonely country."

"Yes, practically desert. But then it would have to be, wouldn't it?"

"You mean so as to leave no trace?"

"Yes. One realises, doesn't one, that the whole thing must be very carefully thought out. Each stage of our journey is, as it were, quite independent of the other. A plane goes up in flames. An old station wagon drives through the night. If anyone notices it, it has on it a plate stating that it belongs to a certain archaeological Expedition that is excavating in these parts. The following day there is a touring car full of Berbers, one of the commonest sights on the road to be seen. For the next stage—" he shrugged his shoulders "—who knows?"

"But where are we going?"

Andy Peters shook his head.

"No use to ask. We shall find out."

The Frenchman, Dr. Barron, had joined them.

"Yes," he said, "we shall find out. But how true it is that we cannot but ask? That is our western blood We can never say 'sufficient for the day.' It is always tomorrow, tomorrow with us. To leave yesterday behind, to proceed to tomorrow. That is what we demand."

"You want to hurry the world on, Doctor, is that it?" asked Peters.

"There is so much to achieve," said Dr. Barron, "life is too short. One must have more time. More time, more time." He flung out his hands in a passionate gesture.

Peters turned to Hilary.

"What are the four freedoms you talk about in your country? Freedom from want, freedom from fear . . ."

The Frenchman interrupted. "Freedom from fools," he said bitterly. "That is what *I* want! That is what my work needs. Freedom from incessant, pettifogging economies! Freedom from all the nagging restrictions that hamper one's work!"

"You are a bacteriologist, are you not, Dr. Barron?"

"Yes, I am a bacteriologist. Ah, you have no idea, my friend, what a fascinating study that is! But it needs patience, infinite patience, repeated experiment—and *money*—much money! One must have equipment, assistants, raw materials! Given that you have all you ask for, what can one not achieve?"

"Happiness?" asked Hilary.

He flashed her a quick smile, suddenly human again.

"Ah, you are a woman, Madame. It is women who ask always for happiness."

"And seldom get it?" asked Hilary.

He shrugged his shoulders.

"That may be."

"Individual happiness does not matter," said Peters seriously, "there must be the happiness of *all*, the brotherhood of the spirit! The workers, free and united, owning the means of production, free of the warmongers, of the greedy, insatiable men who keep everything in their own hands. Science is for *all*, and must not be held jealously by one power or the other."

"So!" said Ericsson appreciatively, "you are right. The scientists must be masters. They must control and rule. They and they alone are the Supermen. It is only the Supermen who matter. The slaves must be well treated, but they *are* slaves."

Hilary walked a little way away from the group. After a minute or two Peters followed her.

"You look just a little scared," he said humorously.

"I think I am." She gave a short, breathless laugh. "Of course what Dr. Barron said was quite true. I'm only a woman. I'm not a scientist, I don't do research or surgery, or bacteriology. I haven't, I suppose, much mental ability. I'm looking, as Dr. Barron said, for happiness—just like any other fool of a woman."

"And what's wrong with that?" said Peters.

"Well, maybe I feel a little out of my depth in this company. You see, I'm just a woman who's going to join her husband."

"Good enough," said Peters. "You represent the fundamental."

"It's nice of you to put it that way."

"Well, it's true." He added in a lower voice, "You care for your husband very much?"

"Would I be here if I didn't?"

"I suppose not. You share his views? I take it that he's a Communist?"

Hilary avoided giving a direct answer.

"Talking of being a Communist," she said, "has something about our little group struck you as curious?"

"What's that?"

"Well, that although we're all bound for the same destination, the views of our fellow travellers don't seem really alike."

Peters said thoughtfully,

"Why, no. You've got something there. I hadn't thought of it quite that way—but I believe you're right."

"I don't think," said Hilary, "that Dr. Barron is politically minded at all! He wants money for his experiments. Helga Needheim talks like a Fascist, not a Communist. And Ericsson—"

"What about Ericsson?"

"I find him frightening—he's got a dangerous kind of single-mindedness. He's like a mad scientist in a film!"

"And I believe in the Brotherhood of men, and you're a loving wife, and our Mrs. Calvin Baker—where would you place her?"

"I don't know. I find her more hard to place than anyone."

"Oh, I wouldn't say that. I'd say she was easy enough."

"How do you mean?"

"I'd say it was money all the way with her. She's just a well-paid cog in the wheel."

"She frightens me, too," said Hilary.

"Why? Why on earth does *she* frighten you? No touch of the mad scientist about her."

"She frightens me because she's so ordinary. You know, just like anybody else. And yet she's mixed up in all this."

Peters said grimly,

"The Party is realistic, you know. It employs the best man or woman for the job."

"But is someone who only wants money the best person for the job? Mightn't they desert to the other side?"

"That would be a very big risk to take," said Peters, quietly. "Mrs. Calvin Baker's a shrewd woman. I don't think she'd take that risk."

Hilary shivered suddenly.

"Cold?"

"Yes. It is a bit cold."

"Let's move around a little."

They walked up and down. As they did so Peters stooped and picked up something.

"Here. You're dropping things."

Hilary took it from him.

"Oh, yes, it's a pearl from my choker. I broke it the other day—no, yesterday. What ages ago that seems already."

"Not real pearls, I hope."

Hilary smiled.

"No, of course not. Costume jewellery."

Peters took a cigarette case from his pocket.

"Costume jewellery," he said, "what a term!"

He offered her a cigarette.

"It does sound foolish—here." She took a cigarette. "What an odd case. How heavy it is."

"Made of lead, that's why. It's a war souvenir—made out of a bit of a bomb that just failed to blow me up."

"You were—in the war then?"

"I was one of the backroom boys who tickled things to see if they'd go bang! Don't let's talk about wars. Let's concentrate on tomorrow."

"Where are we going?" asked Hilary. "Nobody's told me anything. Are we—"

He stopped her.

"Speculations," he said, "are not encouraged. You go where you're told and do what you're told."

With sudden passion Hilary said,

"Do you like being dragooned, being ordered about, having no say of your own?"

"I'm prepared to accept it if it's necessary. And it is necessary. We've got to have World Peace, World Discipline, World Order."

"Is it possible? Can it be got?"

"Anything's better than the muddle we live in. Don't you agree to that?"

For a moment, carried away by fatigue, by the loneliness of her surroundings and the strange beauty of the early morning light, Hilary nearly burst out into a passionate denial.

She wanted to say,

"Why do you decry the world we live in? There are good people in it. Isn't muddle a better breeding ground for kindliness and individuality than a world order that's imposed, a world order that may be right today and wrong tomorrow? I would rather have a world of kindly, faulty, human beings, than a world of superior robots who've said goodbye to pity and understanding and sympathy."

But she restrained herself in time. She said instead, with a deliberate subdued enthusiasm,

"How right you are. I was tired. We must obey and go forward."

He grinned.

"That's better."

10

A DREAM JOURNEY. So it seemed; more so every day. It was as though, Hilary felt, she had been travelling all her life with these five strangely assorted companions. They had stepped off from the beaten track into the void. In one sense this journey of theirs could not be called a flight. They were all, she supposed, free agents; free, that is, to go where they chose. As far as she knew they had committed no crime, they were not wanted by the police. Yet great pains had been taken to hide their tracks. Sometimes she wondered why this was, since they were not fugitives. It was as though they were in process of becoming not themselves but someone else.

That indeed was literally true in her case. She who had left England as Hilary Craven had become Olive Betterton, and perhaps her strange feeling of unreality had something to do with that. Every day the glib political slogans seemed to come more easily to her lips. She felt herself becoming earnest and intense, and that again she put down to the influence of her companions.

She knew now that she was afraid of them. She had never before spent any time in close intimacy with people of genius. This was genius at close quarters, and genius had that something above normal in it that was a great strain upon the ordinary mind and feeling. All five were different from each other, yet each had that curious quality of burning intensity, the single-mindedness of purpose that made such a terrifying impression. She did not know whether it was a quality of brain or rather a quality of outlook, of intensity. But each of them, she thought, was in his or her way a passionate idealist. To Dr. Barron life was a passionate desire to be once more in his laboratory, to be able to calculate and experiment and work with unlimited money and unlimited resources. To work for what? She doubted if he ever put that question to himself. He spoke to her once of the powers of destruction that he could let loose on a vast continent, which could be contained in one little phial. She had said to him,

"But could you ever *do* that? Actually really do it?"

And he replied, looking at her with faint surprise,

"Yes. Yes, of course, if it became necessary."

He had said it in a merely perfunctory fashion. He had gone on,

"It would be amazingly interesting to see the exact course, the exact progress." And he had added with a deep half sigh, "You see, there's so much more to know, so much more to find out."

For a moment Hilary understood. For a moment she stood where he stood, impregnated with that single hearted desire for knowledge which swept aside life and death for millions of human beings as essentially unimportant. It was a point of view and in a way a not ignoble one. Towards Helga Needheim she felt more antagonistic. The young woman's superb arrogance revolted her. Peters she liked but was from time to time repulsed and frightened by the sudden fanatical gleam in his eye. She said to him once,

"It is not a new world you want to create. It is destroying the old one that you will enjoy."

"You're wrong, Olive. What a thing to say."

"No, I'm not wrong. There's hate in you. I can feel it. Hate. The wish to destroy."

Ericsson she found the most puzzling of all. Ericsson, she thought, was a dreamer, less practical than the Frenchman, further removed from destructive passion than the American. He had the strange, fanatical idealism of the Norseman.

"We must conquer," he said, "we must conquer the world. Then we can rule."

"We?" she asked.

He nodded, his face strange and gentle with a deceptive mildness about the eyes.

"Yes," he said, "we few who count. The brains. That is all that matters."

Hilary thought, where are we going? Where is all this leading? These people are mad, but they're not mad in the same way as each other. It's as though they were all going towards different goals, different mirages. Yes, that was the word. *Mirages.* And from them she turned to a contemplation of Mrs. Calvin Baker. Here there was no fanaticism, no hate, no dream, no arrogance, no aspiration. There was nothing here that Hilary could find or take notice of. She was a woman, Hilary thought, without either heart or conscience. She was the efficient instrument in the hands of a big unknown force.

It was the end of the third day. They had come to a small town and alighted at a small native hotel. Here, Hilary found, they were to resume European clothing. She slept that night in a small, bare, whitewashed room, rather like a cell. At early dawn Mrs. Baker woke her.

"We're going off right now," said Mrs. Baker. "The plane's waiting."

"The plane?"

"Why yes, my dear. We're returning to civilized travelling, thank the Lord."

They came to the airfield and the plane after about an hour's drive. It looked like a disused army airfield.

The pilot was a Frenchman. They flew for some hours, their flight taking them over mountains. Looking down from the plane Hilary thought what a curious sameness the world has, seen from above. Mountains, valleys, roads, houses. Unless one was really an aerial expert all places looked alike. That in some the population was denser than in others, was about all that one could say. And half of the time one saw nothing owing to travelling over clouds.

In the early afternoon they began to lose height and circle down. They were in mountainous country still but coming down in a flat plain. There was a well-marked aerodrome here and a white building beside it. They made a perfect landing.

Mrs. Baker led the way towards the building. Beside it were two powerful cars with chauffeurs standing by them. It was clearly a private aerodrome of some kind, since there appeared to be no official reception.

"Journey's end," said Mrs. Baker cheerfully. "We all go in and have a good wash and brush up. And then the cars will be ready."

"Journey's end?" Hilary stared at her. "But we've not—we haven't crossed the sea at all."

"Did you expect to?" Mrs. Baker seemed amused. Hilary said confusedly,

"Well, yes. Yes, I did. I thought . . ." She stopped. Mrs. Baker nodded her head.

"Why, so do a lot of people. There's a lot of nonsense talked about the iron curtain, but what I say is an iron curtain can be anywhere. People don't think of that."

Two Berber servants received them. After a wash and freshening up they sat down to coffee and sandwiches and biscuits. Then Mrs. Baker glanced at her watch.

"Well, so long, folks," she said. "This is where I leave you."

"Are you going back to Morocco?" asked Hilary, surprised.

"That wouldn't quite do," said Mrs. Calvin Baker, "with me being supposed to be burnt up in a plane accident! No, I shall be on a different run this time."

"But someone might still recognise you," said Hilary. "Someone, I mean, who'd met you in hotels in Casablanca or Fez."

"Ah," said Mrs. Baker, "but they'd be making a mistake. I've got a different passport now, though it's true enough that a sister of mine, a Mrs. Calvin Baker, lost her life that way. My sister and I are supposed to be very alike." She added, "And to the casual people one comes across in hotels one travelling American woman is very like another."

Yes, Hilary thought, that was true enough. All the outer, unimportant characteristics were present in Mrs. Baker. The neatness, the trimness, the carefully arranged blue hair, the highly monotonous, prattling voice. Inner characteristics, she realised, were carefully masked or, indeed, absent. Mrs. Calvin Baker presented to the world and to her companions a façade, but what was behind the façade was not easy to fathom. It was as though she had deliberately extinguished those tokens of individuality by which one personality is distinguishable from another.

Hilary felt moved to say so. She and Mrs. Baker were standing a little apart from the rest.

"One doesn't know," said Hilary, "in the least what you're really like."

"Why should you?"

"Yes. Why should I? And yet, you know, I feel I ought to. We've travelled together in rather intimate circumstances and it seems odd to me that I know nothing about you. Nothing, I mean, of the essential you, of what you feel and think, of what you like and dislike, of what's important to you and what isn't."

"You've such a probing mind, my dear," said Mrs. Baker. "If you'll take my advice, you'll curb that tendency."

"I don't even know what part of the United States you come from."

"That doesn't matter either. I've finished with my own country. There are reasons why I can never go back there. If I can pay off a grudge against that country, I'll enjoy doing it."

For just a second or two malevolence showed both in her expression and in the tone of her voice. Then it relaxed once more into cheerful tourist tones.

"Well, so long, Mrs. Betterton, I hope you have a very agreeable reunion with your husband."

Hilary said helplessly,

"I don't even know where I am, what part of the world, I mean."

"Oh, that's easy. There needs to be no concealment about that now. A remote spot in the High Atlas my dear. That's near enough—"

Mrs. Baker moved away and started saying goodbye to the others. With a final gay wave of her hand she walked out across the tarmac. The plane had been refuelled and the pilot was standing waiting for her. A faint cold chill went over Hilary. Here, she felt, was her last link with the outside world. Peters, standing near her, seemed to sense her reaction.

"The place of no return," he said softly. "That's us, I guess."

Dr. Barron said softly,

"Have you still courage, Madame, or do you at this moment want to run after your American friend and

climb with her into the plane and go back—back to the world you have left?"

"Could I go if I wanted to?" asked Hilary.

The Frenchman shrugged his shoulders.

"One wonders."

"Shall I call to her?" asked Andy Peters.

"Of course not," said Hilary sharply.

Helga Needheim said scornfully,

"There is no room here for women who are weaklings."

"She is not a weakling," said Dr. Barron softly, "but she asks herself questions as any intelligent woman would do." He stressed the word "intelligent" as though it were a reflection upon the German woman. She, however, was unaffected by his tone. She despised all Frenchmen and was happily assured of her own worth. Ericsson said, in his high nervous voice,

"When one has at last reached freedom, can one even contemplate going back?"

Hilary said,

"But if it is not possible to go back, or to choose to go back, then it is not freedom!"

One of the servants came to them and said,

"If you please, the cars are ready now to start."

They went out through the opposite door of the building. Two Cadillac cars were standing there with uniformed chauffeurs. Hilary indicated a preference for sitting in front with the chauffeur. She explained the swinging motion of a large car occasionally made her feel car sick. This explanation seemed to be accepted easily enough. As they drove along Hilary made a little desultory conversation from time to time. The weather, the excellence of the car. She spoke French quite easily and well, and the chauffeur responded agreeably. His manner was entirely natural and matter of fact.

"How long will it take us?" she asked presently.

"From the aerodrome to the hospital? It is a drive of perhaps two hours, Madame."

The words struck Hilary with faintly disagreeable surprise. She had noted, without thinking much about it, that Helga Needheim had changed at the rest house and was now wearing a hospital nurse's kit. This fitted in.

"Tell me something about the hospital," she said to the chauffeur.

His reply was enthusiastic.

"Ah, Madame, it is magnificent. The equipment, it is the most up-to-date in the world. Many doctors come and visit it, and all of them go away full of praise. It is a great thing that is being done there for humanity."

"It must be," said Hilary, "yes, yes, indeed it must."

"These miserable ones," said the chauffeur, "they have been sent in the past to perish miserably on a lonely island. But here this new treatment of Dr. Kolini's cures a very high percentage. Even those who are far gone."

"It seems a lonely place to have a hospital," said Hilary.

"Ah, Madame, but you would have to be lonely in the circumstances. The authorities would insist upon it. But it is good air here, wonderful air. See, Madame, you can see now where we are going." He pointed.

They were approaching the first spurs of a mountain range, and on the side of it, set flat against the hillside, was a long gleaming white building.

"What an achievement," said the chauffeur, "to raise such a building out here. The money spent must have been fantastic. We owe much, Madame, to rich philanthropists of this world. They are not like governments who do things always in a cheap way. Here money has been spent like water. Our patron, he is one of the richest men in the world, they say. Here truly he has built a magnificent achievement for the relief of human suffering."

He drove up a winding track. Finally they came to rest outside great barred iron gates.

"You must dismount here, Madame," said the chauffeur. "It is not permitted that I take the car through these gates. The garages are a kilometre away."

The travellers got out of the car. There was a big bell pull at the gate, but before they could touch it the gates swung slowly open. A white-robed figure with a black, smiling face bowed to them and bade them enter. They passed through the gate; at one side screened by a high fence of wire, there was a big courtyard where men were walking up and down. As these men turned to look at the arrivals, Hilary uttered a gasp of horror.

"But they're lepers!" she exclaimed. "Lepers!"

A shiver of horror shook her entire frame.

11

THE GATES OF THE LEPER COLONY closed behind
the travellers with a metallic clang. The noise struck
on Hilary's startled consciousness with a horrible note
of finality. *Abandon hope,* it seemed to say, *all ye who
enter here* . . . This, she thought, was the end . . .
really the end. Any way of retreat there might have
been was now cut off.

She was alone now amongst enemies, and in, at
most, a very few minutes, she would be confronted with
discovery and failure. Subconsciously, she supposed,
she had known that all day, but some undefeatable
optimism of the human spirit, some persistence in the
belief that that entity oneself could not possibly cease
to exist, had been masking that fact from her. She had
said to Jessop in Casablanca "And when do I reach
Tom Betterton?" and he had said then gravely that
that was when the danger would become acute. He
had added that he hoped that by then he might be in
a position to give her protection, but that hope, Hilary
could not but realise, had failed to materialise.

If "Miss Hetherington" had been the agent on whom
Jessop was relying, "Miss Hetherington" had been out-
manoeuvred and left to confess failure at Marrakesh.
But in any case, what could Miss Hetherington have
done?

The party of travellers had arrived at the place of
no return. Hilary had gambled with death and lost.
And she knew now that Jessop's diagnosis had been

correct. She no longer wanted to die. She wanted to live. The zest of living had come back to her in full strength. She could think of Nigel, of the little mound that was Brenda's grave, with a sad wondering pity, but no longer with the cold lifeless despair that had urged her on to seek oblivion in death. She thought: "I'm alive again, sane, whole . . . and now I'm like a rat in a trap. If only there were some way out. . . ."

It was not that she had given no thought to the problem. She had. But it seemed to her, reluctantly, that once confronted with Betterton, there could be no way out. . . .

Betterton would say: "But that's not my wife—" And that would be that! Eyes turning towards her . . . realisation . . . a spy in their midst. . . .

Because what other solution could there be? Supposing she were to get in first? Supposing she were to cry out, before Tom Betterton could get in a word— "Who are you? You're not my husband!" If she could simulate indignation, shock, horror, sufficiently well— might it, just credibly, raise a doubt? A doubt whether Betterton was Betterton—or some other scientist sent to impersonate him. A spy, in other words. But if they believed that, then it might be rather hard on Betterton! But, she thought, her mind turning in tired circles, if Betterton was a traitor, a man willing to sell his country's secrets, could anything be 'hard on him'? How difficult it was, she thought, to make any appraisement of loyalties—or indeed any judgements of people or things. . . . At any rate it might be worth trying. To create a doubt—

With a giddy feeling, she returned to her immediate surroundings. Her thoughts had been running underground with the frenzied violence of a rat caught in a trap. But during that time her surface stream of consciousness had been playing its appointed part.

The little party from the outside world had been welcomed by a big handsome man—a linguist, it would seem, since he had said a word or two to each person in his or her own language.

"Enchanté de faire votre connaissance, mon cher docteur," he was murmuring to Dr. Barron, and then turning to her:

"Ah, Mrs. Betterton, we're very pleased to welcome you here. A long confusing journey, I'm afraid. Your husband's very well and, naturally, awaiting you with impatience."

He gave her a discreet smile; it was a smile, she noticed, that did not touch his cold pale eyes.

"You must," he added, "be longing to see him."

The giddiness increased—she felt the group round her approaching and receding like the waves of the sea. Beside her, Andy Peters put out an arm and steadied her.

"I guess you haven't heard," he said to their welcoming host. "Mrs. Betterton had a bad crash at Casablanca—concussion. This journey's done her no good. Nor the excitement of looking forward to meeting her husband. I'd say she ought to lie down right now in a darkened room."

Hilary felt the kindness of his voice, of the supporting arm. She swayed a little more. It would be easy, incredibly easy, to crumble at the knees, to drop flaccidly down . . . to feign unconsciousness—or at any rate near unconsciousness. Te be laid on a bed in a darkened room—to put off the moment of discovery just a little longer. . . . But Betterton would come to her there—any husband would. He would come there and lean over the bed in the dim gloom and at the first murmur of her voice, the first dim outline of her face as his eye became accustomed to the twilight he would realise that she was not Olive Betterton.

Courage came back to Hilary. She straightened up. Colour came into her cheeks. She flung up her head.

If this were to be the end, let it be a gallant end! She would go to Betterton and when he repudiated her, she would try out the last lie, come out with it confidently, fearlessly.

"No, of course I'm not your wife. Your wife—I'm terribly sorry, it's awful—she's dead. I was in hospital with her when she died. I promised her I'd get to you somehow and give her your last messages. I wanted to. You see, I'm in sympathy with what you did—with what all of you are doing. I agree with you politically. I want to help. . . ."

Thin, thin, all very thin . . . And such awkward trifles to explain—the fake passport—the forged letter of credit. Yes, but people did get by sometimes with the most audacious lies—if one lied with sufficient confidence—if you had the personality to put a thing over. One could at any rate go down fighting.

She drew herself up, gently freeing herself from Peters' support.

"Oh, no. I must see Tom," she said. "I must go to him—now—at once—please."

The big man was hearty about it. Sympathetic. (Though the cold eyes were still pale and watchful.)

"Of course, of course, Mrs. Betterton. I quite understand how you are feeling. Ah, here's Miss Jennsen."

A thin spectacled girl had joined them.

"Miss Jennsen, meet Mrs. Betterton, Fraulein Needheim, Dr. Barron, Mr. Peters, Dr. Ericsson. Show them into the Registry, will you? Give them a drink. I'll be with you in a few minutes. Just take Mrs. Betterton along to her husband. I'll be with you again shortly."

He turned to Hilary again, saying:

"Follow me, Mrs. Betterton."

He strode forward, she followed. At a bend in the

passage, she gave a last look over her shoulder. Andy Peters was still watching her. He had a faintly puzzled unhappy look—she thought for a moment he was going to come with her. He must have realised, she thought, that there's something wrong, realised it from *me,* but he doesn't know what it is.

And she thought, with a slight shiver: "It's the last time, perhaps, that I'll ever see him. . . ."

And so, as she turned the corner after her guide, she raised a hand and waved a goodbye. . . .

The big man was talking cheerfully.

"This way, Mrs. Betterton. I'm afraid you'll find our building rather confusing at first, so many corridors, and all rather alike."

Like a dream, Hilary thought, a dream of hygienic white corridors along which you pass forever, turning, going on, never finding your way out. . . .

She said:

"I didn't realise it would be a—a hospital."

"No, no, of course. You couldn't realise anything, could you?"

There was a faint sadistic note of amusement in his voice.

"You've had, as they say, to 'fly blind.' My name's Van Heidem, by the way. Paul Van Heidem."

"It's all a little strange—and rather terrifying," said Hilary. "The lepers . . ."

"Yes, yes, of course. Picturesque—and usually so very unexpected. It does upset newcomers. But you'll get used to them—oh yes, you'll get used to them in time."

He gave a slight chuckle.

"A very good joke, I always think myself."

He paused suddenly.

"Up one flight of stairs—now don't hurry. Take it easy. Nearly there now."

Nearly there—nearly there . . . so many steps to

death . . . up—up—deep steps, deeper than European steps. And now another of the hygienic passages and Van Heidem was stopping by a door. He tapped, waited, and then opened it.

"Ah, Betterton—here we are at last. Your wife!"

He stood aside with a slight flourish.

Hilary walked into the room. No holding back. No shrinking. Chin up. Forward to doom.

A man stood half turned from the window, an almost startlingly good-looking man. She noted that, recognising his fair handsomeness with a feeling almost of surprise. He wasn't, somehow, her idea of Tom Betterton. Surely, the photograph of him that she had been shown wasn't in the least—

It was that confused feeling of surprise that decided her. She would go all out for her desperate expedient.

She made a quick movement forward, then drew back. Her voice rang out, startled, dismayed . . .

"But—that isn't Tom. That isn't my husband. . . ."

It was well done, she felt it herself. Dramatic, but not over dramatic. Her eyes met Van Heidem's in bewildered questioning.

And then Tom Betterton laughed. A quiet, amused, almost triumphant laugh.

"Pretty good, eh, Van Heidem?" he said, "if even my own wife doesn't know me!"

With four quick steps he had crossed to her and gathered her tightly into his arms.

"Olive, darling. Of course you know me. I'm Tom all right even if I haven't got quite the same face as I used to have."

His face pressed against hers, his lips by her ear, she caught the faint whispered addition,

"Play up. For God's sake. Danger."

He released her for a moment, caught her to him again.

"Darling! It's seemed years—years and years. But you're here at last!"

She could feel the warning pressure of his fingers below her shoulder blades, admonishing her, giving their urgent message.

Only after a moment or two did he release her, push her a little from him and look into her face.

"I still can't quite believe it," he said with an excited little laugh. "Still, you know it's me now, don't you?"

His eyes, burning into hers, still held that message of warning.

She didn't understand it—couldn't understand it. But it was a miracle from heaven and she rallied to play her part.

"Tom!" she said, and there was a catch in her voice that her listening ears approved. "Oh, Tom—but what—"

"Plastic surgery! Hertz of Vienna is here. And he's a living marvel. Don't say you regret my old crushed nose."

He kissed her again, lightly, easily, this time, then turned to the watching Van Heidem with a slight apologetic laugh.

"Forgive the transports, Van," he said.

"But naturally, naturally—" the Dutchman smiled benevolently.

"It's been so long," said Hilary, "and I—" she swayed a little, "I—please, can I sit down."

Hurriedly Tom Betterton eased her into a chair.

"Of course, darling. You're all in. That frightful journey. And the plane accident. My God, what an escape!"

(So there was full communication. They knew all about the plane crash.)

"It's left me terribly woolly-headed," said Hilary, with an apologetic little laugh. "I forget things and get muddled up, and have awful headaches. And then, finding you looking like a total stranger, I'm a bit of a mess, darling. I hope I won't be a bother to you!"

"You a bother? Never. You'll just have to take it easy for a bit, that's all. There's all the—time in the world here."

Van Heidem moved gently towards the door.

"I will leave you now," he said. "After a little you will bring your wife to the Registry, Betterton? For the moment you will like to be left alone."

He went out, shutting the door behind him.

Immediately Betterton dropped on his knees by Hilary and buried his face on her shoulder.

"Darling, darling," he said.

And once again she felt that warning pressure of the fingers. The whisper, so faint as hardly to be heard, was urgent and insistent.

"Keep it up. There might be a microphone—one never knows."

That was it, of course. One never knew. . . . Fear—uneasiness—uncertainty—danger—always danger—she could feel it in the atmosphere.

Tom Betterton sat back on his haunches.

"It's so wonderful to see you," he said softly. "And yet, you know, it's like a dream—not quite real. Do you feel like that, too?"

"Yes, that's just it—a dream—being here—with you—at last. It doesn't seem real, Tom."

She had placed both hands on his shoulders. She was looking at him, a faint smile on her lips. (There might be a spy hole as well as a microphone.)

Coolly and calmly she appraised what she saw. A nervous good-looking man of thirty-odd who was badly frightened—a man nearly at the end of his tether—a man who had, presumably, come here full of high hopes and had been reduced—to this.

Now that she had surmounted her first hurdle, Hilary felt a curious exhilaration in the playing of her part. She must *be* Olive Betterton. Act as Olive would have acted, feel as Olive would have felt. And life was so unreal that that seemed quite natural. Somebody called Hilary Craven had died in an aeroplane accident. From now on she wouldn't even remember her.

Instead, she rallied her memories of the lessons she had studied so assiduously.

"It seems such ages since Firbank," she said. "Whiskers—you remember Whiskers? She had kittens—just after you went away. There are so many things, silly everyday little things, you don't even know about. That's what seemed so odd."

"I know. It's breaking with an old life and beginning a new one."

"And—it's all right here? You're happy?"

A necessary wifely question that any wife would ask.

"It's wonderful." Tom Betterton squared his shoulders, threw his head back. Unhappy, frightened eyes looked out of a smiling confident face. "Every facility. No expense spared. Perfect conditions to get on with the job. And the organisation! It's unbelievable."

"Oh, I'm sure it is. My journey—did you come the same way?"

"One doesn't talk about that. Oh, I'm not snubbing you, darling. But—you see, you've got to learn about everything."

"But the lepers? Is it really a Leper Colony?"

"Oh yes. Perfectly genuine. There's a team of medicos doing very fine work in research on the subject. But it's quite self-contained. It needn't worry you. It's just—clever camouflage."

"I see." Hilary looked around her. "Are these our quarters?"

"Yes. Sitting room, bathroom there, bedroom beyond. Come, I'll show you."

She got up and followed him through a well-appointed bathroom into a good-sized bedroom with twin beds, big built-in cupboards, a dressing table, and a bookshelf near the beds. Hilary looked into the cupboard space with some amusement.

"I hardly know what I'm going to put in here," she remarked. "All I've got is what I stand up in."

"Oh that. You can fit yourself out with all you want. There's a fashion model department and all accessories, cosmetics, everything. All first class. The Unit is quite self-contained—all you want on the premises. No need to go outside ever again."

He said the words lightly, but it seemed to Hilary's sensitive ear that there was despair concealed behind the words.

No need to go outside ever again. No chance of ever going outside again. *Abandon hope all ye who enter here* . . . The well-appointed cage! Was it for this, she thought, that all these varying personalities had abandoned their countries, their loyalties, their everyday lives? Dr. Barron, Andy Peters, young Ericsson with his dreaming face, the overbearing Helga Needheim? Did they know what they were coming to find? Would they be content? Was this what they had wanted?

She thought: "I'd better not ask too many questions . . . If someone is listening."

Was someone listening? Were they being spied upon? Tom Betterton evidently thought it might be so. But was he right?

Or was it nerves—hysteria? Tom Betterton, she thought, was very near to a breakdown.

"Yes," she thought firmly, "and so may you be, my girl, in six months' time . . ."

What did it do to people, she wondered, living like this?

Tom Betterton said to her:

"Would you like to lie down—to rest?"

"No—" she hesitated. "No, I don't think so."

"Then perhaps you'd better come with me to the Registry."

"What's the Registry?"

"Everyone who clocks in goes through the Registry. They record everything about you. Health, teeth, blood pressure, blood group, psychological reactions, tastes, dislikes, allergies, aptitudes, preferences."

"It sounds very military—or do I mean medical?"

"Both," said Tom Betterton. "Both. This organisation—it's really formidable."

"One's always heard so," said Hilary. "I mean that everything behind the Iron Curtain is really properly planned."

She tried to put a proper enthusiasm into her voice. After all, Olive Betterton had presumably been a sympathiser with the Party, although, perhaps by order, she had not been known to be a Party member.

Betterton said evasively,

"There's a lot for you to—understand," He added quickly: "Better not try to take in too much at once."

He kissed her again, a curious, apparently tender and even passionate kiss, that was actually cold as ice, murmured very low in her ear, "Keep it up," and said aloud, "And now, come down to the Registry."

12

THE REGISTRY was presided over by a woman who looked like a strict nursery governess. Her hair was rolled into a rather hideous bun and she wore some very efficient-looking pince-nez. She nodded approval as the Bettertons entered the severe office-like room.

"Ah," she said, "You've brought Mrs. Betterton. That's right."

Her English was perfectly idiomatic but it was spoken with a stilted precision which made Hilary believe that she was probably a foreigner. Actually, her nationality was Swiss. She motioned Hilary to a chair, opened a drawer beside her and took out a sheaf of forms upon which she commenced to write rapidly. Tom Betterton said rather awkwardly:

"Well then, Olive, I'll leave you."

"Yes, please, Dr. Betterton. It's much better to get through all the formalities straight away."

Betterton went out, shutting the door behind him. The Robot, for such Hilary thought of her, continued to write.

"Now then," she said, in a businesslike way. "Full name, please. Age. Where born. Father's and mother's names. Any serious illnesses. Tastes. Hobbies. List of any jobs held. Degrees at any universities. Preferences in food and drink."

It went on, a seemingly endless catalogue. Hilary responded vaguely, almost mechanically. She was glad now of the careful priming she had received from Jessop. She had mastered it all so well that the responses came automatically, without having to pause or think. The Robot said finally, as she made the last entry,

"Well, that seems to be all for this department. Now we'll hand you over to Dr. Schwartz for medical examination."

"Really!" said Hilary. "Is all this necessary? It seems most absurd."

"Oh, we believe in being thorough, Mrs. Betterton. We like to have everything down in the records. You'll like Dr. Schwartz very much. Then from her you go on to Dr. Rubec."

Dr. Schwartz was fair and amiable and female. She gave Hilary a meticulous physical examination and then said,

"So! That is finished. Now you go to Dr. Rubec."

"Who is Dr. Rubec?" Hilary asked. "Another doctor?"

"Dr. Rubec is a psychologist."

"I don't want a psychologist. I don't like psychologists."

"Now please don't get upset, Mrs. Betterton. You're not going to have treatment of any kind. It's simply a question of an intelligence test and of your type-group personality."

Dr. Rubec was a tall, melancholy Swiss of about forty years of age. He greeted Hilary, glanced at the card that had been passed on to him by Dr. Schwartz and nodded his head approvingly.

"Your health is good, I am glad to see," he said. "You have had an aeroplane crash recently, I understand?"

"Yes," said Hilary. "I was four or five days in hospital at Casablanca."

"Four or five days are not enough," said Dr. Rubec reprovingly. "You should have been there longer."

"I didn't want to be there longer. I wanted to get on with my journey."

"That, of course, is understandable, but it is important with concussion that plenty of rest should be had. You may appear quite well and normal after it but it may have serious effects. Yes, I see your nerve reflexes are not quite what they should be. Partly the excitement of the journey and partly, no doubt, due to concussion. Do you get headaches?"

"Yes. Very bad headaches. And I get muddled up every now and then and can't remember things."

Hilary felt it well to continually stress this particular point. Dr. Rubec nodded soothingly.

"Yes, yes, yes. But do not trouble yourself. All that will pass. Now we will have a few association tests, so as to decide what type of mentality you are."

Hilary felt faintly nervous but all appeared to pass off well. The tests seemed to be of a merely routine nature. Dr. Rubec made various entries on a long form.

"It is a pleasure," he said at last, "to deal with someone (if you will excuse me, Madam, and not to take amiss what I am going to say), to deal with someone who is not in any way a genius!"

Hilary laughed.

"Oh, I'm certainly not a genius," she said.

"Fortunately for you," said Dr. Rubec. "I can assure you your existence will be far more tranquil." He sighed. "Here, as you probably understand, I deal mostly with keen intellects, but with the type of sensitive intellect that is apt to become easily unbalanced, and where the emotional stress is strong. The man of science, Madame, is not the cool, calm individual he is made out to be in fiction. In fact," said Dr. Rubec, thoughtfully, "between a first-class tennis player, an operatic prima-donna and a nuclear physicist there is really very little difference as far as emotional instability goes."

"Perhaps you are right," said Hilary, remembering that she was supposed to have lived for some years in close proximity to scientists. "Yes, they *are* rather temperamental sometimes."

Dr. Rubec threw up a pair of expressive hands.

"You would not believe," he said, "the emotions that arise here! The quarrels, the jealousies, the *touchiness!* We have to take steps to deal with all that. But you, Madame," he smiled. "You are in a class that is in a small minority here. A fortunate class, if I may so express myself."

"I don't quite understand you. What kind of a minority?"

"Wives," said Dr. Rubec. "We have not many wives here. Very few are permitted. One finds them, on the whole, refreshingly free from the brainstorms of their husbands and their husbands' colleagues."

"What do wives do here?" asked Hilary. She added apologetically, "You see it's all so new to me. I don't understand anything yet."

"Naturally not. Naturally. That is bound to be the case. There are hobbies, recreations, amusements, instructional courses. A wide field. You will find it, I hope, an agreeable life."

"As you do?"

It was a question, and rather an audacious one and Hilary wondered a moment or two later whether she had been wise to ask it. But Dr. Rubec merely seemed amused.

"You are quite right, Madame," he said. "I find life here peaceful and interesting in the extreme."

"You don't ever regret—Switzerland?"

"I am not homesick. No. That is partly because, in my case, my home conditions were bad. I had a wife and several children. I was not cut out, Madame, to be a family man. Here conditions are infinitely more pleasant. I have ample opportunity of studying certain aspects of the human mind which interest me and on which I am writing a book. I have no domestic cares, no distractions, no interruptions. It all suits me admirably."

"And where do I go next?" asked Hilary, as he rose and shook her courteously and formally by the hand.

"Mademoiselle La Roche will take you to the dress department. The result, I am sure—" he bowed "—will be admirable."

After the severe Robotlike females she had met so far, Hilary was agreeably surprised by Mademoiselle La Roche. Mademoiselle La Roche had been a *vendeuse* in one of the Paris houses of *haute couture* and her manner was thrillingly feminine.

"I am delighted, Madame, to make your acquaintance. I hope that I can be of assistance to you. Since you have just arrived and since you are, no doubt, tired, I would suggest that you select now just a few essentials. Tomorrow and indeed during the course of next week, you can examine what we have in stock at your leisure. It is tiresome I always think, to have to select things rapidly. It destroys all the pleasure of *la toilette*. So I would suggest, if you agree, just a set of underclothing, a dinner dress, and perhaps a *tailleur*."

"How delightful it sounds," said Hilary. "I cannot tell you how odd it feels to own nothing but a toothbrush and a sponge."

Mademoiselle La Roche laughed cheeringly. She took a few rapid measures and led Hilary into a big apartment with built-in cupboards. There were clothes here of every description, made of good material and excellent cut and in a large variety of sizes. When Hilary had selected the essentials of *la toilette*, they passed on to the cosmetics department where Hilary made a selection of powders, creams and various other toilet accessories. These were handed to one of the assistants, a native girl with a shining dark face, dressed in spotless white, and she was instructed to see that they were delivered to Hilary's apartment.

All these proceedings had seemed to Hilary more and more like a dream.

"And we shall have the pleasure of seeing you again shortly, I hope," said Mademoiselle La Roche, gracefully. "It will be a great pleasure, Madame, to assist you to select from our models. *Entre. nous* my work is sometimes disappointing. These scientific ladies often take very little interest in *la toilette.* In fact, not a half hour ago I had a fellow traveller of yours."

"Helga Needheim?"

"Ah yes, that was the name. She is of course, a *Boche,* and the *Boches* are not sympathetic to us. She is not actually bad looking if she took a little care of her figure; if she chose a flattering line she could look very well. But no! She has no interest in clothes. She is a doctor, I understand. A specialist of some kind. Let us hope she takes more interest in her patients than she does in her *toilette*—Ah, that one, what man will look at her twice?"

Miss Jennsen, the thin, dark, spectacled girl who had met the party on arrival, now entered the fashion salon.

"Have you finished here, Mrs. Betterton?" she asked.

"Yes, thank you," said Hilary.

"Then perhaps you will come and see the Deputy Director."

Hilary said "au revoir" to Mademoiselle La Roche and followed the earnest Miss Jennsen.

"Who is the Deputy Director?" she asked.

"Doctor Nielson."

Everybody, Hilary reflected, in this place was doctor of something.

"Who exactly is Doctor Nielson?" she asked. "Medical, scientific, what?"

"Oh, he's not medical, Mrs. Betterton. He's in charge of Administration. All complaints have to go to him. He's the administrative head of the Unit. He always has an interview with everyone when they arrive. After that I don't suppose you'll ever see him again unless something very important should arise."

"I see," said Hilary meekly. She had an amused feeling of having been put severely in her place.

Admission to Dr. Nielson was through two antechambers where stenographers were working. She and her guide were finally admitted into the inner sanctum where Dr. Nielson rose from behind a large executive's desk. He was a big florid man with an urbane manner. Of trans-Atlantic origin, Hilary thought, though he had very little American accent.

"Ah!" he said, rising and coming forward to shake Hilary by the hand. "This is—yes—let me see—yes, Mrs. Betterton. Delighted to welcome you here, Mrs. Betterton. We hope you'll be very happy with us. Sorry to hear of the unfortunate accident during the course of your journey, but I'm glad it was no worse. Yes, you were lucky there. Very lucky indeed. Well, your husband's been awaiting you impatiently and I hope now you've got here you will settle down and be very happy amongst us."

"Thank you, Dr. Nielson."

Hilary sat down in the chair he drew forward for her.

"Any questions you want to ask me?" Dr. Nielson leant forward over his desk in an encouraging manner.

Hilary laughed a little.

"That's a most difficult thing to answer," she said. "The real answer is, of course, that I've got so many questions to ask that I don't know where to begin."

"Quite, quite. I understand that. If you'll take my advice—this is just advice, you know, nothing more—I shouldn't ask anything. Just adapt yourself and see what comes. That's the best way, believe me."

"I feel I know so little," said Hilary. "It's all so—so very unexpected."

"Yes. Most people think that. The general idea seems to have been that one was going to arrive in Moscow." He laughed cheerfully. "Our desert home is quite a surprise to most people."

"It was certainly a surprise to me."

"Well, we don't tell people too much beforehand. They mightn't be discreet, you know, and discretion's rather important. But you'll be comfortable here, you'll find. Anything you don't like—or particularly would like to have . . . just put in a request for it and we'll see what can be managed. Any artistic requirement, for instance. Painting, sculpture, music, we have a department for all that sort of thing."

"I'm afraid I'm not talented that way."

"Well, there's plenty of social life too, of a kind. Games, you know. We have tennis courts, squash courts. It takes a week or two, we often find, for people to find their feet, especially the wives, if I may say so. Your husband's got his job and he's busy with it and it takes a little time, sometimes, for the wives to find—well—other wives who are congenial. All that sort of thing. You understand me."

"But does one—does one—stay here?"

"Stay here? I don't quite understand you, Mrs. Betterton."

"I mean, does one stay here or go on somewhere else?"

Dr. Nielson became rather vague.

"Ah," he said. "That depends on your husband. Ah, yes, yes, that depends very much on him. There are possibilities. Various possibilities. But it's better not to go into all that just now. I'd suggest, you know, that you—well—come and see me again perhaps in three weeks' time. Tell me how you've settled down. All that kind of thing."

"Does one—go out at all?"

"Go out, Mrs. Betterton?"

"I mean outside the walls. The gates."

"A very natural question," said Dr. Nielson. His manner was now rather heavily beneficent. "Yes, very natural. Most people ask it when they come here. But the point of our Unit is that it's a world in itself. There is nothing, if I may so express myself, to go out *to*. Outside us there is only desert. Now I'm not blaming you, Mrs. Betterton. Most people feel like that when they first get here. Slight claustrophobia. That's how Dr. Rubec puts it. But I assure you that it passes off. It's a hangover, if I may so express it, from the world that you have left. Have you ever observed an ant hill, Mrs. Betterton? An interesting sight. Very interesting and very instructive. Hundreds of little black insects hurrying to and fro, so earnest, so eager, so purposeful. And yet the whole thing's such a muddle. That's the bad old world you have left. Here there is leisure, purpose, infinite time. I assure you," he smiled, "an earthly paradise."

13

"IT'S LIKE A SCHOOL," said Hilary.

She was back once more in her own *suite*. The clothes and accessories she had chosen were awaiting her in the bedroom. She hung the clothes in the cupboards and arranged the other things to her liking.

"I know," said Betterton, "I felt like that at first."

Their conversation was wary and slightly stilted. The shadow of a possible microphone still hung over them. He said in an oblique manner,

"I think it's all right, you know. I think I was probably imagining things. But all the same . . ."

He left it at that, and Hilary realised that what he had left unsaid was, "but all the same, we had better be careful."

The whole business was, Hilary thought, like some fantastic nightmare. Here she was, sharing a bedroom with a strange man, and yet so strong was the feeling of uncertainty, and danger, that to neither of them did the intimacy appear embarrassing. It was like, she thought, climbing a Swiss mountain where you share a hut in close proximity with guides and other climbers as a matter of course. After a minute or two Betterton said,

"It all takes a bit of getting used to, you know. Let's just be very natural. Very ordinary. More or less as if we were at home still."

She realised the wisdom of that. The feeling of unreality persisted and would persist, she supposed, some little time. The reasons for Betterton leaving England, his hopes, his disillusionment could not be touched upon between them at this moment. They were two people playing a part with an undefined menace hanging over them, as it were. She said presently,

"I was taken through a lot of formalities. Medical, psychological and all that."

"Yes. That's always done. It's natural I suppose."

"Did the same happen to you?"

"More or less."

"Then I went in to see the—Deputy Director I think they called him?"

"That's right. He runs this place. Very capable and a thoroughly good administrator."

"But he's not really the head of it all?"

"Oh no, there's the Director himself."

"Does one—do I—shall I see the Director?"

"Sooner or later I expect. But he doesn't often appear. He gives us an address from time to time—he's got a wonderfully stimulating personality."

There was a faint frown between Betterton's brows and Hilary thought it wise to abandon the subject. Betterton said, glancing at a watch,

"Dinner is at eight. Eight to eight-thirty, that is. We'd better be getting down, if you're ready?"

He spoke exactly as though they were staying in a hotel.

Hilary had changed into the dress she had selected. A soft shade of grey-green that made a good background for her red hair. She clasped a necklace of rather attractive costume jewellery round her neck and said she was ready. They went down the stairs and along corridors and finally into a large dining room. Miss Jennsen came forward and met them.

"I have arranged a slightly larger table for you, Tom," she said to Betterton. "A couple of your wife's fellow travellers will sit with you—and the Murchisons, of course."

They went along to the table indicated. The room contained mostly small tables seating four, eight or ten persons. Andy Peters and Ericsson were already sitting at the table and rose as Hilary and Tom approached. Hilary introduced her "husband" to the two men. They sat down, and presently they were joined by another couple. These Betterton introduced as Dr. and Mrs. Murchison.

"Simon and I work in the same lab," he said, in an explanatory fashion.

Simon Murchison was a thin, anaemic-looking young man of about twenty-six. His wife was dark and stocky. She spoke with a strong foreign accent and was, Hilary gathered, an Italian. Her Christian name was Bianca. She greeted Hilary politely but, or so it seemed to Hilary, with a certain reserve.

"Tomorrow," she said, "I will show you around the place. You are not a scientist, no?"

"I'm afraid," said Hilary, "that I have had no scientific training." She added, "I worked as a secretary before my marriage."

"Bianca has had legal training," said her husband. "She has studied economics and commercial law. Sometimes she gives lectures here but it is difficult to find enough to do to occupy one's time."

Bianca shrugged her shoulders.

"I shall manage," she said. "After all, Simon, I came here to be with you and I think that there is much here that could be better organised. I am studying conditions. Perhaps Mrs. Betterton, since she will not be engaged on scientific work, can help me with these things."

Hilary hastened to agree to this plan. Andy Peters made them all laugh by saying ruefully,

"I guess I feel rather like a homesick little boy who's

just gone to boarding school. I'll be glad to get down to doing some work."

"It's a wonderful place for working," said Simon Murchison with enthusiasm. "No interruptions and all the apparatus you want."

"What's your line?" asked Andy Peters.

Presently the three men were talking a jargon of their own which Hilary found difficult to follow. She turned to Ericsson who was leaning back in his chair, his eyes abstracted.

"And you?" she asked. "Do you feel like a homesick little boy too?"

He looked at her as though from a long way away.

"I do not need a home," he said. "All these things; home, ties of affection, parents, children; all these are a great hindrance. To work one should be quite free."

"And you feel that you will be free here?"

"One cannot tell yet. One hopes so."

Bianca spoke to Hilary.

"After dinner," she said, "there is a choice of many things to do. There is a card room and you can play bridge; or there is a cinema or three nights a week theatrical performances are given and occasionally there is dancing."

Ericsson frowned disapprovingly.

"All these things are unnecessary," he said. "They dissipate energy."

"Not for us women," said Bianca. "For us women they are necessary."

He looked at her with an almost cold and impersonal dislike.

Hilary thought: "To him women are unnecessary, too."

"I shall go to bed early," said Hilary. She yawned deliberately. "I don't think I want to see a film or play bridge this evening."

"No, dear," said Tom Betterton hastily. "Much better to go to bed really early and have a good night's rest. You've had a very tiring journey, remember."

As they rose from the table, Betterton said:

"The air here is wonderful at night. We usually take a turn or two on the roof garden after dinner, before dispersing to recreations or study. We'll go up there for a little and then you'd better go to bed."

They went up in a lift manned by a magnificent-looking native in white robes. The attendants were darker-skinned and of more massive build than the slighter Berbers—a desert type, Hilary thought. She was startled by the unexpected beauty of the roof garden, and also by the lavish expenditure that must have gone to create it. Tons of earth must have been brought and carried up here. The result was like an Arabian Nights fairy tale. There was the plash of water, tall palms, the tropical leaves of bananas and other plants and paths of beautiful coloured tiles with designs of Persian flowers.

"It's unbelievable," said Hilary. "Here in the middle of the desert." She spoke out what she had felt: "It's an Arabian Nights fairy tale."

"I agree with you, Mrs. Betterton," said Murchison. "It looks exactly as though it has come into being by conjuring up a Djin! Ah well—I suppose even in the desert there's nothing you can't do, given water and money—plenty of both of them."

"Where does the water come from?"

"Spring tapped deep in the mountain. That's the *raison d'être* of the Unit."

A fair sprinkling of people was on the roof garden, but little by little they dwindled away. The Murchisons excused themselves. They were going to watch some ballet.

There were few people left now. Betterton guided Hilary with his hand on her arm to a clear space near the parapet. The stars showed above them and the air was cold now, crisp and exhilarating. They were alone here. Hilary sat down on the low concrete, and Betterton stood in front of her.

"Now then," he said in a low nervous voice, *"Who the hell are you?"*

She looked up at him for a moment or two without answering. Before she replied to his question there was something that she herself had got to know.

"Why did you recognise me as your wife?" she asked.

They looked at each other. Neither of them wished to be the first to answer the other's question. It was a duel of wills between them, but Hilary knew that whatever Tom Betterton had been like when he left England, his will was now inferior to her own. She had arrived here fresh in the self-confidence of organising her own life— Tom Betterton had been living a planned existence. She was the stronger.

He looked away from her at last, and muttered sullenly:

"It was—just an impulse. I was probably a damned fool. I fancied that you might have been sent—to get me out of here."

"You want to get out of here, then?"

"My God, can you ask?"

"How did you get here from Paris?"

Tom Betterton gave a short unhappy laugh.

"I wasn't kidnapped or anything like that, if that's what you mean. I came of my own free will, under my own steam. I came keenly and enthusiastically."

"You knew that you were coming here?"

"I'd no idea I was coming to Africa, if that's what you mean. I was caught by the usual lure. Peace on earth, free sharing of scientific secrets amongst the scientists of the world; suppression of capitalists and warmongers—all the usual jargon! That fellow Peters who came with you is the same, he's swallowed the same bait."

"And when you got here—it wasn't like that?"

Again he gave that short bitter laugh.

"You'll see for yourself. Oh, perhaps it *is* that, more or less! But it's not the way you thought it would be. It's not—*freedom*."

He sat down beside her frowning to himself.

"That's what got me down at home, you know. The feeling of being watched and spied upon. All the security precautions. Having to account for one's actions, for one's friends . . . All necessary, I daresay, but it gets you down in the end . . . And so when someone comes along with a proposition—well, you listen . . . It all sounds fine . . ." He gave a short laugh. "And one ends up—here!"

Hilary said slowly:

"You mean you've come to exactly the same circumstances as those from which you tried to escape? You're being watched and spied upon in just the same way—or worse?"

Betterton pushed his hair back nervously from his forehead.

"I don't know," he said. "Honestly. I don't know. I can't be sure. It may be all going on in my own mind. I don't know that I'm being watched at all. Why should I be? Why should they bother? They've got me here—in prison."

"It isn't in the least as you imagined it?"

"That's the odd thing. I suppose it *is* in a way. The working conditions are perfect. You've every facility, every kind of apparatus. You can work for as long a time as you like or as short a time. You've got every comfort and accessory. Food, clothes, living quarters, but you're conscious all the time that you're in prison."

"I know. When the gates clanged behind us today as we came in it was a horrible feeling." Hilary shuddered.

"Well," Betterton seemed to pull himself together. "I've answered your question. Now answer mine. What are you doing here pretending to be Olive?"

"Olive—" she stopped, feeling for words.

"Yes? What about Olive? What's happened to her? What are you trying to say?"

She looked with pity at his haggard nervous face.

"I've been dreading having to tell you."

"You mean—something's happened to her?"

"Yes. I'm sorry, terribly sorry. . . . Your wife's dead. . . . She was coming to join you and the plane crashed. She was taken to hospital and died two days later."

He stared straight ahead of him. It was as though he was determined to show no emotion of any kind. He said quietly:

"So Olive's dead? I see . . ."

There was a long silence. Then he turned to her.

"All right. I can go on from there. You took her place and came here, why?"

This time Hilary was ready with her response. Tom Betterton had believed that she had been sent "to get him out of here" as he had put it. That was not the case. Hilary's position was that of a spy. She had been sent to gain information not to plan the escape of a man who had placed himself willingly in the position he now was. Moreover she could command no means of deliverance, she was a prisoner as much as he was.

To confide in him fully would, she felt, be dangerous. Betterton was very near a breakdown. At any moment he might go completely to pieces. In those circumstances it would be madness to expect him to keep a secret.

She said,

"I was in the hospital with your wife when she died.

I offered to take her place and try and reach you. She wanted to get a message to you very badly."

He frowned.

"But surely—"

She hurried on—before he could realise the weakness of the tale.

"It's not so incredible as it sounds. You see I had a lot of sympathy with all these ideas—the ideas you've just been talking about. Scientific secrets shared with all nations—a new World Order. I was enthusiastic about it all. And then my hair—if what they expected was a red-haired woman of the right age, I thought I'd get through. It seemed worth trying anyway."

"Yes," he said. His eyes swept over her head. "Your hair's exactly like Olive's."

"And then, you see, your wife was so insistent— about the message she wanted me to give to you."

"Oh yes, the message. What message?"

"To tell you to be careful—very careful—that you were in danger—from someone called Boris?"

"Boris? Boris Glydr, do you mean?"

"Yes, do you know him?"

He shook his head.

"I've never met him. But I know him by name. He's a relation of my first wife's. I know about him."

"Why should he be dangerous?"

"What?"

He spoke absently.

Hilary repeated her question.

"Oh, that." He seemed to come back from far away. "I don't know why he should be dangerous to *me,* but it's true that by all accounts he's a dangerous sort of chap."

"In what way?"

"Well, he's one of those half balmy idealists who

would quite happily kill off half humanity if they thought for some reason it would be a good thing."

"I know the sort of person you mean."

She felt she did know—vividly. (But why?)

"Had Olive seen him? What did he say to her?"

"I can't tell you. That's all she said. About danger— oh yes, she said she couldn't believe it."

"Believe what?"

"I don't know." She hesitated a minute and then said, "You see—she was dying . . ."

A spasm of pain convulsed his face.

"I know . . . I know . . . I shall get used to it in time. At the moment I can't realise it. But I'm puzzled about Boris. How could he be dangerous to me *here*? If he'd seen Olive he was in London, I suppose?"

"He was in London, yes."

"Then I simply don't get it. . . . Oh well, what does it matter? What the hell does anything matter? Here we are, stuck in this bloody Unit surrounded by a lot of inhuman Robots . . ."

"That's just how they felt to me."

"And we can't get out." He pounded with his fist on the concrete. *"We can't get out."*

"Oh yes, we can," said Hilary.

He turned to stare at her in surprise.

"What on earth do you mean?"

"We'll find a way," said Hilary.

"My dear girl," his laugh was scornful. "You haven't the faintest idea what you're up against in this place."

"People escaped from the most impossible places during the war," said Hilary stubbornly. She was not going to give in to despair. "They tunnelled, or something."

"How can you tunnel through sheer rock? And where to? It's desert all round."

"Then it will have to be 'or something.' "

He looked at her. She smiled with a confidence that was dogged rather than genuine.

"What an extraordinary girl you are. You sound quite sure of yourself."

"There's always a way. I daresay it will take time, and a lot of planning."

His face coloured over again.

"Time," he said. "Time . . . That's what I can't afford."

"Why?"

"I don't know whether you'll be able to understand . . . It's like this. I can't really—do my stuff here."

She frowned.

"How do you mean?"

"How shall I put it? I can't work. I can't *think*. In my stuff one has to have a high degree of concentration. A lot of it is—well—*creative*. Since coming here I've just lost the urge. All I can do is good sound hack work. The sort of thing any two-penny-halfpenny scientific chap can do. But that's not what they brought me here for. They want original stuff and I can't *do* original stuff. And the more nervous and afraid I get, the less I'm fit to turn out anything worth turning out. And it's driving me off my rocker, do you see?"

Yes, she saw now. She recalled Dr. Rubec's remarks about prima donnas and scientists.

"If I can't deliver the goods, what is an outfit like this going to do about it? They'll liquidate me."

"Oh no."

"Oh yes they will. They're not sentimentalists here. What's saved me so far is this plastic surgery business. They do it a little at a time, you know. And naturally a fellow who's having constant minor operations can't be expected to concentrate. But they've finished the business now."

"But why was it done at all? What's the point?"

"Oh, that! For safety. My safety, I mean. It's done if —if you're a 'wanted' man."

"Are you a 'wanted' man, then?"

"Yes, didn't you know? Oh, I suppose they wouldn't advertise the fact in the papers. Perhaps even Olive didn't know. But I'm wanted right enough."

"You mean for—*treason* is the word, isn't it? You mean you've sold them atom secrets?"

He avoided her eyes.

"I didn't sell anything. I gave them what I knew of our processes—gave it freely. If you can believe me, I *wanted* to give it to them. It was part of the whole setup —the pooling of scientific knowledge. Oh, can't you understand?"

She could understand. She could understand Andy Peters doing just that. She could see Ericsson with his fanatical dreamer's eyes betraying his country with a high-souled enthusiasm.

Yet it was hard for her to visualise Tom Betterton doing it—and she realised with a shock that all that showed was the difference between Betterton a few months ago, arriving in all the zeal of enthusiasm, and Betterton now, nervous, defeated, down to earth—an ordinary badly frightened man.

Even as she accepted the logic of that, Betterton looked round him nervously and said:

"Everyone's gone down. We'd better—"

She rose.

"Yes. But it's all right, you know. They'll think it quite natural—under the circumstances."

He said awkwardly:

"We'll have to go on with this now, you know. I mean—you'll have to go on being—my wife."

"Of course."

"And we'll have to share a room and all that. But it

will be quite all right. I mean, you needn't be afraid that—"

He swallowed in an embarrassed manner.

"How handsome he is," thought Hilary, looking at his profile, "and how little it moves me . . ."

"I don't think we need worry about that," she said cheerfully. "The important thing is to get out of here alive."

14

In a room at the Hotel Mamounia, Marrakesh, the man called Jessop was talking to Miss Hetherington. A different Miss Hetherington this, from the one that Hilary had known at Casablanca and at Fez. The same appearance, the same twin set, the same depressing hair-do. But the manner had changed. It was a woman now both brisk, competent, and seeming years younger than her appearance.

The third person in the room was a dark stocky man with intelligent eyes. He was tapping gently on the table with his fingers and humming a little French song under his breath.

". . . and as far as you know," Jessop was saying, "those are the only people she talked to at Fez?"

Janet Hetherington nodded.

"There was the Calvin Baker woman, whom we'd already met at Casablanca. I'll say frankly I still can't make up my mind about her. She went out of her way to be friendly with Olive Betterton, and with me for that matter. But Americans are friendly, they do enter into conversation with people in hotels, and they like joining them on trips."

"Yes," said Jessop, "it's all a little too overt for what we're looking for."

"And besides," went on Janet Hetherington, *"she* was on this plane, too."

"You're assuming," said Jessop, "that the crash was
157

planned." He looked sideways towards the dark, stocky man. "What about it, Leblanc?"

Leblanc stopped humming his tune, and stopped his little tattoo on the table for a moment or two.

"*Ça se peut*," he said. "There may have been sabotage to the machine and that is why it crashed. We shall never know. The plane crashed and went up in flames and everyone on board was killed."

"What do you know of the pilot?"

"Alcadi? Young, reasonably competent. No more. Badly paid." He added the last two words with a slight pause in front of them.

Jessop said:

"Open therefore to other employment, but presumably not a candidate for suicide?"

"There were seven bodies," said Leblanc. "Badly charred, unrecognisable, but seven bodies. One cannot get away from that."

Jessop turned back to Janet Hetherington.

"You were saying?" he said.

"There was a French family at Fez that Mrs. Betterton exchanged a few words with. There was a rich Swedish business man with a glamour girl. And the rich old magnate, Mr. Aristides."

"Ah," said Leblanc, "that fabulous figure himself. What must it feel like, I have often asked myself, to have all the money in the world? For me," he added frankly, "I would keep race horses and women, and all the world has to offer. But old Aristides shuts himself up in his castle in Spain—literally his castle in Spain, *mon cher*—and collects, so they say, Chinese potteries of the Sung period. But one must remember," he added, "that he is at least seventy. It is possible at that age that Chinese potteries are all that interest one."

"According to the Chinese themselves," said Jessop, "the years between sixty and seventy are the most rich in living and one is then most appreciative of the beauty and delight of life."

"Pas moi!" said Leblanc.

"There were some Germans at Fez, too," continued Janet Hetherington, "but as far as I know they didn't exchange any remarks with Olive Betterton."

"A waiter or a servant, perhaps," said Jessop.

"That's always possible."

"And she went out into the old town alone, you say?"

"She went with one of the regular guides. Someone may have contacted her on that tour."

"At any rate she decided quite suddenly to go to Marrakesh."

"Not suddenly," she corrected him. "She already had her reservations."

"Ah, I'm wrong," said Jessop. "What I mean is that Mrs. Calvin Baker decided rather suddenly to accompany her." He got up and paced up and down. "She flew to Marrakesh," he said, "and the plane crashed and came down in flames. It seems ill-omened, does it not, for anyone called Olive Betterton to travel by air. First the crash near Casablanca, and then this one. Was it an accident or was it contrived? If there were people who wished to get rid of Olive Betterton, there would be easier ways to do it than wrecking a plane, I should say."

"One never knows," said Leblanc. "Understand me, *mon cher*. Once you have got into that state of mind where the taking of human lives no longer counts, then if it is simpler to put a little explosive package under a seat in a plane, than to wait about at the corner on a dark night and stick a knife into someone, then the package will be left and the fact that six other people will die also is not even considered."

"Of course," said Jessop, "I know I'm in a minority

of one, but I still think there's a third solution—that they faked the crash."

Leblanc looked at him with interest.

"That could be done, yes. The plane could be brought down and it could be set on fire. But you cannot get away from the fact, *mon cher* Jessop, that there were *people* in the plane. The charred bodies were actually *there*."

"I know," said Jessop. "That's the stumbling block. Oh, I've no doubt my ideas are fantastic, but it's such a neat ending to our hunt. Too neat. That's what I feel. It says finish to us. We write down R.I.P. in the margin of our report and it's ended. There's no further trail to take up." He turned again to Leblanc. "You are having that search instituted?"

"For two days now," said Leblanc. "Good men, too. It's a particularly lonely spot, of course, where the plane crashed. It was off its course, by the way."

"Which is significant," Jessop put in.

"The nearest villages, the nearest habitations, the nearest traces of a car, all those are being investigated fully. In this country as well as in yours, we fully realise the importance of the investigation. In France, too, we have lost some of our best young scientists. In my opinion, *mon cher,* it is easier to control temperamental opera singers than it is to control a scientist. They are brilliant, these young men, erratic, rebellious; and finally and dangerously, they are most completely credulous. What do they imagine goes on *là-bas?* Sweetness and light and desire for truth and the millennium? Alas, poor children, what disillusionment awaits them."

"Let's go over the passenger list once more," said Jessop.

The Frenchman reached out a hand, picked it out of a wire basket and set it before his colleague. The two men pored over it together.

"Mrs. Calvin Baker, American. Mrs. Betterton, English. Torquil Ericsson, Norwegian—what do you know of him, by the way?"

"Nothing that I can recall," said Leblanc. "He was young, not more than twenty-seven or twenty-eight."

"I know his name," said Jessop, frowning. "I think—I am almost sure—that he read a paper before the Royal Society."

"Then there is the *religieuse*," Leblanc said, turning back to the list. "Sister Marie something or other. Andrew Peters, also American. Dr. Barron. That is a celebrated name, *le docteur Barron*. A man of great brilliance. An expert on virus diseases."

"Biological warfare," said Jessop. "It fits. It all fits."

"A man poorly paid and discontented," said Leblanc.

"How many going to St. Ives?" murmured Jessop.

The Frenchman shot him a quick look and he smiled apologetically.

"Just an old nursery rhyme," he said. "For St. Ives read question mark. Journey to nowhere."

The telephone on the table buzzed and Leblanc picked up the receiver.

"Allo?" he said. *"Qu'est ce qu'il y a?* Ah, yes, send them up." He turned his head towards Jessop. His face was suddenly alive, vigorous. "One of my men reporting," he said. "They have found something. *Mon cher collègue,* it is possible—I say no more—possible that your optimism is justified."

A few moments later two men entered the room. The first bore a rough resemblance to Leblanc, the same type, stocky, dark, intelligent. His manner was respectful but exhilarated. He wore European clothes badly stained and marked, covered with dust. He had obviously just arrived from a journey. With him was a native wearing the white local dress. He had the dignified composure of the dweller in remote places. His manner was courteous but not subservient. He looked with a faint wonder round the room whilst the other man explained things in rapid French.

"The reward was offered and circulated," the man explained, "and this fellow and his family and a great many of his friends have been searching diligently. I let him bring you the find himself as there may be questions you want to ask him."

Leblanc turned to the Berber—

"You have done good work," he said, speaking now in the man's own language. "You have the eyes of the hawk, my father. Show us then what you have discovered."

From a fold in his white robe the man took out a small object, and stepping forward laid it on the table before the Frenchman. It was rather a large sized pinkish grey synthetic pearl.

"It is like the one shown to me and shown to others," he said. "It is of value and I have found it."

Jessop stretched out a hand and took the pearl. From his pocket he drew out another exactly like it and examined both. Then he walked across the room to the window, and examined them both through a powerful lens.

"Yes," he said, "the mark is there." There was jubilation now in his voice and he came back to the table. "Good girl," he said, "good girl, good girl! She managed it!"

Leblanc was questioning the Berber in a rapid exchange of Arabic. Finally he turned to Jessop.

"I make my apologies, *mon cher collègue*," he said. "This pearl was found at a distance of nearly *half a mile* from the flaming plane."

"Which shows," said Jessop, "that Olive Betterton was a survivor, and that though seven people left Fez in the plane and seven charred bodies were found, one of those charred bodies was definitely not hers."

"We extend the search now," said Leblanc. He spoke again to the Berber and the man smiled back happily. He left the room with the man who had brought him in. "He will be handsomely rewarded as promised," said Leblanc, "and there will be a hunt now all over the countryside for these pearls. They have hawk eyes, these people, and the knowledge that these are worth good money in reward will pass round like a grapevine. I think—I think, *mon cher collègue,* that we shall get results! If only they have not tumbled to what she was doing."

Jessop shook his head.

"It would be such a natural occurrence," he said. "The sudden breaking of a necklace of costume jewellery such as most women wear, the picking up apparently of what loose pearls she can find and stuffing them into her pocket, then a little hole in the pocket. Besides, why should they suspect her? She is Olive Betterton, anxious to join her husband."

"We must review this matter in a new light," said Leblanc. He drew the passenger list towards him. "Olive Betterton. Dr. Barron," he said, ticking off the two names. "Two at least who are going—wherever they are going. The American woman, Mrs. Calvin Baker. As to her we keep an open mind. Torquil Ericsson you say has read papers before the Royal Society. The American, Peters, was described on his passport as a Research Chemist. The *religieuse*—well, it would make a good disguise. In fact, a whole cargo of people cleverly shepherded from different points to travel in that one plane on that particular day. And then the plane is discovered in flames and inside it the requisite number of charred bodies. How did they manage that, I wonder? *Enfin, c'est colossal!"*

"Yes," said Jessop. "It was the final convincing touch. But we know now that six or seven people have started off on a fresh journey, and we know where their point of departure is. What do we do next—visit the spot?"

"But precisely," said Leblanc. "We take up advanced headquarters. If I mistake not, now that we are on the track, other evidence will come to light.

"If our calculations are exact," Leblanc said, "there should be results."

The calculations were many and devious. The rate of progress of a car, the likely distance where it would refuel, possible villages where travellers might have stayed the night. The tracks were many and confusing, disappointments were continual, but every now and then there came a positive result.

"Voilà, mon capitaine! A search of the latrines, as you ordered. In a dark corner of the latrine a pearl embedded in a little piece of chewing gum in the house of one Abdul Mohammed. He and his sons have been interrogated. At first they denied, but at last they have confessed. A carload of six people said to be from the German archaeological expedition spent a night in his house. Much money was paid, and they were not to mention this to anyone, the excuse being that there was some illicit digging in prospect. Children in the village of El Kaif also have brought in two more pearls. We know now the direction. There is more, *Monsieur le Capitaine.* The hand of Fatima has been seen as you foretold. This type here, he will tell you about it."

"This type" was a particularly wild-looking Berber.

"I was with my flocks," he said, "at night and I heard a car. It passed me as it did so I saw the sign. The hand of Fatima was outlined on one side of it. It gleamed, I tell you, in the darkness."

"The application of phosphorous on a glove can be

very efficacious," murmured Leblanc. "I congratulate you, *mon cher,* on that idea."

"It's effective," said Jessop, "but it's dangerous. It's too easily noticed by the fugitives themselves, I mean."

Leblanc shrugged his shoulders.

"It could not be seen in daylight."

"No, but if there was a halt and they alighted from the car in the darkness—"

"Even then—it is a notable Arab superstition. It is painted often on carts and wagons. It would only be thought that some pious Moslem had painted it in luminous paint on his vehicle."

"True enough. But we must be on our guard. For if our enemies did notice it, it is highly possible that they will lay a false trail for us, of hands of Fatima in phosphorous paint."

"Ah, as to that I agree with you. One must indeed be on one's guard. Always, always on one's guard."

On the following morning Leblanc had another exhibit of three false pearls arranged in a triangle, stuck together by a little piece of chewing gum.

"This should mean," said Jessop, "that the next stage of the journey was by plane." He looked enquiringly at Leblanc.

"You are absolutely right," said the other. "This was found on a disused army airfield, in a remote and desolate place. There were signs that a plane landed and left there not long ago." He shrugged his shoulders. "An unknown plane," he said, "and once again they took off for a destination unknown. That brings us once more to a halt and we do not know where next to take up the trail."

15

"IT'S INCREDIBLE," thought Hilary to herself, "incredible that I've been here ten days!" The frightening thing in life, Hilary thought, was how easily you adapted yourself. She remembered once being shown in France some peculiar torture arrangements of the Middle Ages, an iron cage wherein a prisoner had been confined and in which he could neither lie, stand nor sit. The guide had recounted how the last man imprisoned there had lived in it for eighteen years, had been released and had lived for another twenty after that, before dying, an old man. That adaptability, thought Hilary, was what differentiated man from the animal world. Man could live in any climate and on any food and under any conditions. He could exist slave or free.

She had felt first, when introduced into the Unit, a blinding panic, a horrible feeling of imprisonment and frustration, and the fact that the imprisonment was camouflaged in circumstances of luxury had somehow made it seem all the more horrible to her. And yet now, already, even after a week here she had begun insensibly to accept the conditions of her life as natural. It was a queer, dreamlike existence. Nothing seemed particularly real, but already she had the feeling that the dream had gone on a long time and would go on for a long time more. It would, perhaps, last forever. . . . She would always live here in the Unit, this was life, and there was nothing outside.

This dangerous acceptance, she thought, came partly

from the fact that she was a woman. Women were adaptable by nature. It was their strength and their weakness. They examined their environment, accepted it, and like realists settled down to make the best of it. What interested her most were the reactions of the people who had arrived here with her. Helga Needheim she hardly ever saw except sometimes at meals. When they met, the German woman vouchsafed her a curt nod, but no more. As far as she could judge, Helga Needheim was happy and satisfied. The Unit obviously lived up to the picture she had formed in her mind of it. She was the type of woman absorbed by her work, and was comfortably sustained by her natural arrogance. The superiority of herself and her fellow scientists was the first article of Helga's creed. She had no views of a brotherhood of man, of an era of peace, of liberty of mind and spirit. For her the future was narrow but all conquering. The super race, herself a member of it; the rest of the world in bondage, treated, if they behaved, with condescending kindness. If her fellow workers expressed different views, if their ideas were Communist rather than Fascist, Helga took little notice. If their work was good they were necessary, and their ideas would change.

Dr. Barron was more intelligent than Helga Needheim. Occasionally Hilary had brief conversations with him. He was absorbed in his work, deeply satisfied with the conditions provided for him, but his enquiring Gallic intellect led him to speculate and ponder on the media in which he found himself.

"It was not what I expected. No, frankly," he said one day, *"entre nous,* Mrs. Betterton, I do not care for prison conditions. And these *are* prison conditions, though the cage, let us say, is heavily gilded."

"There is hardly the freedom here that you came to seek?" Hilary suggested.

He smiled at her, a quick, rueful smile.

"But no," he said, "you are wrong. I did not really seek liberty. I am a civilized man. The civilized man knows there is no such thing. Only the younger and cruder nations put the word *Liberty* on their banner. There must always be a planned framework of security. And the essence of civilization is that the way of life should be a moderate one. The middle way. Always one comes back to the middle way. No. I will be frank with you. I came here for money."

Hilary in her turn smiled. Her eyebrows rose.

"And what good is money to you here?"

"It pays for very expensive laboratory equipment," said Dr. Barron. "I am not obliged to put my hand into my own pocket, and so I can serve the cause of science and satisfy my own intellectual curiosity. I am a man who loves his work, true, but I do not love it for the sake of humanity. I have usually found that those who do so are somewhat woolly headed, and often incompetent workers. No, it is the pure intellectual joy of research that I appreciate. For the rest, a large sum of money was paid to me before I left France. It is safely banked under another name and in due course, when all this comes to an end, I shall have it to spend as I choose."

"When all this comes to an end?" Hilary repeated. "But why should it come to an end?"

"One must have the common sense," said Dr. Barron, "nothing is permanent, nothing endures. I have come to the conclusion that this place is run by a madman. A madman, let me tell you, can be very logical. If you are rich and logical and also mad, you can succeed for a very long time in living out your illusion. But in the end —" he shrugged, "—in the end this will break up. Because, you see, it is not reasonable, what happens here!

That which is not reasonable must always pay the reckoning in the end. In the meantime—" again he shrugged his shoulders, "—it suits me admirably."

Torquil Ericsson, whom Hilary expected to be violently disillusioned, appeared to be quite content in the atmosphere of the Unit. Less practical than the Frenchman, he existed in a single-minded vision of his own. The world in which he lived was one so unfamiliar to Hilary that she could not even understand it. It engendered a kind of austere happiness, an absorption in mathematical calculations, and an endless vista of possibilities. The strange, impersonal ruthlessness of his character frightened Hilary. He was the kind of young man, she thought, who in a moment of idealism could send three quarters of the world to their death in order that the remaining quarter should participate in an impractical Utopia that existed only in Ericsson's mind.

With the American, Andy Peters, Hilary felt herself far more in accord. Possibly, she thought, it was because Peters was a man of talents but not a genius. From what others said, she gathered he was a first-class man at his job, a careful and skilled chemist, but not a pioneer. Peters, like herself, had at once hated and feared the atmosphere of the Unit.

"The truth is that I didn't know where I was going," he said. "I thought I knew, but I was wrong. The Party has got nothing to do with this place. We're not in touch with Moscow. This is a lone show of some kind—a Fascist show possibly."

"Don't you think," said Hilary, "that you go in too much for labels?"

He considered this.

"Maybe you're right," he said. "Come to think of it, these words we throw around don't mean much. But I do know this. I want to get out of here and I mean to get out of here."

"It won't be easy," said Hilary, in a low voice.

They were walking together after dinner near the splashing fountains of the roof garden. With the illusion of darkness and the starlit sky they might have been in the private gardens of some sultan's palace. The functional concrete buildings were veiled from their sight.

"No," said Peters, "it won't be easy, but nothing's impossible."

"I like to hear you say that," said Hilary. "Oh, how I like to hear you say that!"

He looked at her sympathetically.

"Been getting you down?" he asked.

"Very much so. But that's not what I'm really afraid of."

"No? what then?"

"I'm afraid of getting used to it," said Hilary.

"Yes." He spoke thoughtfully. "Yes, I know what you mean. There's a kind of mass suggestion going on here. I think perhaps you're right about that."

"It would seem to me much more natural for people to rebel," said Hilary.

"Yes. Yes, I've thought the same. In fact I've wondered once or twice whether there's not a little hocus-pocus going on."

"Hocus-pocus? What do you mean by that?"

"Well, to put it frankly, dope."

"Do you mean a drug of some kind?"

"Yes. It might be possible, you know. Something in the food or drink, something that induces—what shall I say—docility?"

"But is there such a drug?"

"Well, that's not really my line of country. There are things that are given to people to soothe them down, to make them acquiescent before operations and that. Whether there is anything that can be administered steadily over a long period of time—and which at the same time does not impair efficiency—that I don't know. I'm more inclined to think now that the effect is produced mentally. I mean that I think some of these organisers and administrators here are well-versed in hypnosis and psychology and that, without our being aware of it, we are continually being offered suggestions of our well being, of our attaining our ultimate aim (whatever it is), and that all this *does* produce a definite effect. A lot can be done that way, you know, if it's done by people who know their stuff."

"But we mustn't acquiesce," cried Hilary, hotly. "We mustn't feel for one moment that it's a good thing to be here."

"What does your husband feel?"

"Tom? I—oh, I don't know. It's so difficult. I—" she lapsed into silence.

The whole fantasy of her life as she lived it she could hardly communicate to the man who was listening to her. For ten days now she had lived in an apartment with a man who was a stranger to her. They shared a bedroom and when she lay awake at night she could hear him breathing in the other bed. Both of them accepted the arrangement as inevitable. She was an impostor, a spy, ready to play any part and assume any personality. Tom Betterton she quite frankly did not understand. He seemed to her a terrible example of what could happen to a brilliant young man who had lived for some months in the enervating atmosphere of the Unit. At any rate there was in him no calm acceptance of his destiny. Far from taking pleasure in his work, he was, she thought, increasingly worried by his inability to concentrate on it. Once or twice he had reiterated what he had said on the first evening.

"I can't think. It's just as though everything in me has dried up."

Yes, she thought, Tom Betterton, being a real genius,

needed liberty more than most. Suggestion had failed to compensate him for the loss of freedom. Only in perfect liberty was he able to produce creative work.

He was a man, she thought, very close to a serious nervous breakdown. Hilary herself he treated with curious inattention. She was not a woman to him, not even a friend. She even doubted whether he realised and suffered from the death of his wife. The thing that preoccupied him incessantly was the problem of confinement. Again and again he had said,

"I must get away from here. I must, I must." And sometimes, "I didn't know. I'd no idea what it was going to be like. How *am* I going to get out of here? How? I've got to. I've simply got to."

It was in essence very much what Peters had said. But it was said with a great deal of difference. Peters had spoken as a young, energetic, angry, disillusioned man, sure of himself and determined to pit his wits against the brains of the establishment in which he found himself. But Tom Betterton's rebellious utterances were those of a man at the end of his tether, a man almost crazed with the need for escape. But perhaps, Hilary thought suddenly, that was where she and Peters would be in six months' time. Perhaps what began as healthy rebellion and a reasonable confidence in one's own ingenuity, would turn at last into the frenzied despair of a rat in a trap.

She wished she could talk of all this to the man beside her. If only she could say: "Tom Betterton isn't my husband. I know nothing about him. I don't know what he was like before he came here and so I'm in the dark. I can't help him, for I don't know what to do or say." As it was she had to pick her words carefully. She said,

"Tom seems like a stranger to me now. He doesn't— tell me things. Sometimes I think the confinement, the sense of being penned up here, is driving him mad."

"It's possible," said Peters drily, "it could act that way."

"But tell me—you speak so confidently of getting away. How *can* we get away—what earthly chance is there?"

"I don't mean we can walk out the day after tomorrow, Olive. The thing's got to be thought out and planned. People have escaped, you know, under the most unpromising conditions. A lot of our people, and a lot your side of the Atlantic, too, have written books about escape from fortresses in Germany."

"That was rather different."

"Not in essence. Where there's a way in there's a way out. Of course tunnelling is out of the question here, so that knocks out a good many methods. But as I say, where there's a way in, there's a way out. With ingenuity, camouflage, playing a part, deception, bribery and corruption, one ought to manage it. It's the sort of thing you've got to study and think about. I'll tell you this. I *shall* get out of here. Take it from me."

"I believe you will," said Hilary, then she added, "but shall I?"

"Well, it's different for you."

His voice sounded embarrassed. For a moment she wondered what he meant. Then she realised that presumably her own objective had been attained. She had come here to join the man she had loved, and having joined him her own personal need for escape should not be so great. She was almost tempted to tell Peters the truth—but some instinct of caution forbade that.

She said goodnight and left the roof.

16

"GOOD EVENING, Mrs. Betterton."

"Good evening, Miss Jennsen."

The thin spectacled girl was looking excited. Her eyes glinted behind the thick lenses.

"There will be a Reunion this evening," she said. "The *Director himself* is going to address us!"

She spoke in an almost hushed voice.

"That's good," said Andy Peters who was standing close by. "I've been waiting to catch a glimpse of this Director."

Miss Jennsen threw him a glance of shocked reproof.

"The Director," she said austerely, "is a very wonderful man."

As she went away from them down one of the inevitable white corridors, Andy Peters gave a low whistle.

"Now did I, or did I not, catch a hint of the Heil Hitler attitude there?"

"It certainly sounded like it."

"The trouble in this life is that you never really know where you're going. If I'd known when I left the States all full of boyish ardour for the good old Brotherhood of Man that I was going to land myself in the clutches of yet another Heavenborn Dictator—" he threw out his hands.

"You don't know that yet," Hilary reminded him.

"I can smell it—in the air," said Peters.

"Oh," cried Hilary, "how glad I am that you're here." She flushed, as he looked at her quizzically.

"You're so nice and ordinary," said Hilary desperately.

Peters looked amused.

"Where I come from," he said, "the word ordinary doesn't have your meaning. It can stand for being just plain mean."

"You know I didn't mean it that way. I mean you're like everybody else. Oh dear, that sounds rude, too."

"The common man, that's what you're asking for? You've had enough of the genius?"

"Yes, and you've changed, too, since you came here. You've lost that streak of bitterness—of hatred."

But immediately his face grew rather grim.

"Don't count on that," he said. "It's still there—underneath. I can still hate. There are things, believe me, that *should* be hated."

The Reunion, as Miss Jennsen had called it, took place after dinner. All members of the Unit assembled in the large lecture room.

The audience did not include what might be called the technical staff: the laboratory assistants, the corps de ballet, the various service personnel, and the small assembly of handsome prostitutes who also served the Unit as purveyors of sex to those men who had no wives with them and had formed no particular attachments with the female workers.

Sitting next to Betterton, Hilary awaited with keen curiosity the arrival on the platform of that almost mythical figure, the Director. Questioned by her, Tom Betterton had given unsatisfactory, almost vague answers, about the personality of the man who controlled the Unit.

"He's nothing much to look at," he said. "But he has tremendous impact. Actually I've only seen him twice.

He doesn't show up often. He's remarkable, of course, one feels that, but honestly I don't know *why*."

From the reverent way Miss Jennsen and some of the other women spoke about him, Hilary had formed a vague mental picture of a tall man with a golden beard wearing a white robe—a kind of godlike abstraction.

She was almost startled when, as the audience rose to their feet, a dark rather heavily built man of middle age came quietly onto the platform. In appearance he was quite undistinguished, he might have been a business man from the Midlands. His nationality was not apparent. He spoke to them in three languages, alternating one with the other, and never exactly repeating himself. He used French, German and English, and each was spoken with equal fluency.

"Let me first," he began, "welcome our new colleagues who have come to join us here."

He then paid a few words of tribute to each of the new arrivals.

After that he went on to speak of the aims and beliefs of the Unit.

Trying to remember his words later, Hilary found herself unable to do so with any accuracy. Or perhaps it was that the words, as remembered, seemed trite and ordinary. But listening to them was a very different thing.

Hilary remembered once being told by a friend who had lived in Germany in the days before the war, how she had gone to a meeting in mere curiosity to listen "to that absurd Hitler"—and how she had found herself crying hysterically, swept away by intense emotion. She had described how wise and inspiring every word had seemed, and how, afterwards, the remembered words in their actuality had seemed commonplace enough.

Something of the same kind was happening now. In

spite of herself, Hilary was stirred and uplifted. The Director spoke very simply. He spoke primarily of Youth. With Youth lay the future of mankind.

"Accumulated Wealth, Prestige, influential Families —those have been the forces of the past. But today, power lies in the hands of the young. Power is in Brains, The brains of the chemist, the physicist, the doctor . . . From the laboratories comes the power to destroy on a vast scale. With that power you can say 'Yield—or perish!' That power should not be given to this or that nation. Power should be in the hands of those who create it. This Unit is a gathering place for the Power of all the world. You come here from all parts of the globe, bringing with you your creative scientific knowledge. And with you, you bring *Youth!* No one here is over forty-five. When the day comes, we shall create a Trust. The Brains Trust of Science. And we shall administer world affairs. We shall issue our orders to Capitalists and Kings and Armies and Industries. We shall give the World the *Pax Scientifica.*"

There was more of it—all the same heady intoxicating stuff—but it was not the words themselves—it was the power of the orator that carried away an assembly that could have been cold and critical had it not been swayed by that nameless emotion about which so little is known.

When the Director had ended abruptly:

"Courage and Victory! Goodnight!" Hilary left the Hall, half stumbling in a kind of exalted dream, and recognised the same feeling in the faces around her. She saw Ericsson in particular, his pale eyes gleaming, his head tossed back in exultation.

Then she felt Andy Peters' hand on her arm and his voice said in her ear:

"Come up on the roof. We need some air."

They went up in the lift without speaking and stepped

out among the palm trees under the stars. Peters drew a deep breath.

"Yes," he said. "This is what we need. Air to blow away the clouds of glory."

Hilary gave a deep sigh. She still felt unreal.

He gave her arm a friendly shake.

"Snap out of it, Olive."

"Clouds of glory," said Hilary. "You know—it *was* like that!"

"Snap out of it, I tell you. Be a woman! Down to earth and basic realities! When the effects of the Glory Gas poisoning pass off you'll realise that you've been listening to the same old Mixture as Before."

"But it was fine—I mean a fine ideal."

"Nuts to ideals. Take the facts. Youth and Brains— glory glory Alleluia! And what are the youth and brains? Helga Needheim, a ruthless egoist. Torquil Ericsson, an impractical dreamer. Dr. Barron who'd sell his grand-mother to the knacker's yard to get equipment for his work. Take me, an ordinary guy, as you've said your-self, good with the test-tube and the microscope but with no talent whatever for efficient administration of an office, let alone a World! Take your own husband —yes. I'm going to say it—a man whose nerves are frayed to nothing and who can think of nothing but the fear that retribution will catch up with him. I've given you those people we know best—but they're all the same here—or all that I've come across. Geniuses, some of them, damned good at their chosen jobs—but as Administrators of the Universe—hell, don't make me laugh! Pernicious nonsense, that's what we've been listening to."

Hilary sat down on the concrete parapet. She passed a hand across her forehead.

"You know," she said. "I believe you're right . . .

But the clouds of glory are still trailing. How does he do it? Does he believe it himself? He must."

Peters said gloomily,

"I suppose it always comes to the same thing in the end. A madman who believes he's God."

Hilary said slowly,

"I suppose so. And yet—that seems curiously unsatisfactory."

"But it happens, my dear. Again and again throughout history it happens. And it gets one. It nearly got me, tonight. It *did* get you. If I hadn't whisked you up here—" his manner changed suddenly. "I suppose I shouldn't have done that. What will Betterton say? He'll think it odd."

"I don't think so. I doubt if he'll notice."

He looked at her questioningly.

"I'm sorry, Olive. It must be all pretty fair hell for you. Seeing him go down the hill."

Hilary said passionately,

"We must get out of here. We must. We must."

"We shall."

"You said that before—but we've made no progress."

"Oh yes we have. I've not been idle."

She looked at him in surprise.

"No precise plan, but I've initiated subversive activities. There's a lot of dissatisfaction here, far more than our god-like Herr Director knows. Amongst the humbler members of the Unit, I mean. Food and money and luxury and women aren't everything, you know. I'll get you out of here yet, Olive."

"And Tom, too."

Peters' face darkened.

"Listen, Olive, and believe what I say. Tom will do best to stay on here. He's—" he hesitated, "—safer here than he would be in the outside world."

"Safer? What a curious word."

"Safer," said Peters. "I use the word deliberately."

Hilary frowned.

"I don't really see what you mean. Tom's not—you don't think he's becoming mentally unhinged?"

"Not in the least. He's het up, but I'd say Tom Betterton's as sane as you or I."

"Then why are you saying he'd be safer here?"

Peters said slowly,

"A cage you know, is a very safe place to be."

"Oh no," cried Hilary. "Don't tell me you're going to believe that too. Don't tell me that mass hypnotism, or suggestion, or whatever it is, is working on you. Safe, tame, content! We *must* rebel still! We must want to be free!"

Peters said slowly,

"Yes, I know. But—"

"Tom, at any rate, wants desperately to get away from here."

"Tom mayn't know what's good for him."

Suddenly Hilary remembered what Tom had hinted at to her. If he had disposed of secret information he would be liable, she supposed, to prosecution under the Official Secrets Act— That, no doubt, was what Peters was hinting at in his rather embarrassed way—but Hilary was clear in her own mind. Better to serve a prison sentence even than remain on here. She said, obstinately,

"Tom must come, too."

She was startled when Peters said suddenly, in a bitter tone,

"Have it your own way. I've warned you. I wish I knew what the hell makes you care for that fellow so much?"

She stared at him in dismay. Words sprang to her lips, but she checked them. She realised that what she wanted to say was, "I don't care for him. He's nothing to me. He was another woman's husband and I've a responsibility to her." She wanted to say, "You fool, if there's anybody I care about, it's *you* . . ."

2

"Been enjoying yourself with your tame American?"

Tom Betterton threw the words at her as she entered their bedroom. He was lying on his back on his bed, smoking.

Hilary flushed slightly.

"We arrived here together," she said, "and we seem to think alike about certain things."

He laughed.

"Oh I don't blame you." For the first time he looked at her in a new and appraising way. "You're a good-looking woman, Olive," he said.

From the beginning Hilary had urged him always to call her by his wife's name.

"Yes," he continued, his eyes raking her up and down. "You're a damned good-looking woman. I'd have noticed that once. As it is, nothing of that kind seems to register with me any more."

"Perhaps it's just as well," said Hilary drily.

"I'm a perfectly normal man, my dear, or I used to be. God knows what I am now."

Hilary sat down by him.

"What *is* the matter with you, Tom?" she said.

"I tell you, I can't concentrate. As a scientist I'm shot to pieces. This place—"

"The others—or most of them—don't seem to feel like you?"

"Because they're a damned insensitive crowd, I suppose."

"Some of them are temperamental enough," said

Hilary, drily. She went on, "If only you had a friend here—a real friend."

"Well, there's Murchison. Though he's a dull dog. And I've seen a good deal of Torquil Ericsson lately."

"Really?" For some reason Hilary felt surprised.

"Yes. My God, he's brilliant. I wish I had *his* brains."

"He's an odd sort of person," said Hilary. "I always find him rather frightening."

"Frightening? Torquil? He's as mild as milk. Like a child in some ways. No knowledge of the world."

"Well *I* find him frightening," repeated Hilary obstinately.

"Your nerves must be getting upset, too."

"Not yet. I suspect they will, though. Tom—don't get too friendly with Torquil Ericsson."

He stared at her.

"Why ever not?"

"I don't know. It's a feeling I have."

17

LEBLANC SHRUGGED his shoulders.

"They have left Africa, it is certain."

"Not *certain*."

"The probabilities point that way." The Frenchman shook his head. "After all, we know, do we not, for where they are bound?"

"If they are bound for where we think, why start the journey from Africa? Anywhere in Europe would be simpler."

"That is true. But there is the other side of it. No one would expect them to assemble and start from here."

"I still think there's more to it than that." Jessop was gently insistent. "Besides, only a small plane could have used that airfield. It would have to come down and refuel before crossing the Mediterranean. And where they refuelled some trace should have been left."

"*Mon cher*, we have instituted the most searching enquiries—everywhere there has been—"

"The men with the Geiger counters must get results in the end. The number of planes to be examined is limited. Just a trace of radio-activity and we shall know that is the plane we are looking for—"

"If your agent has been able to use the spray. Alas! Always so many 'ifs' . . ."

"We shall get there," said Jessop obstinately. "I wonder—"

"Yes?"

"We have assumed they are going *north*—towards the Mediterranean—suppose instead, they flew *south*."

"Doubled back on their tracks? But where, then, could they be flying *to?* There are the mountains of the High Atlas—and after that the desert sands."

2

"Sidi, you swear to me that it will be as you have promised? A petrol station in America, in Chicago? It is certain?"

"It is certain, Mohammed, if we get out of here, that is."

"Success depends on the will of Allah."

"Let us hope, then, that it is the will of Allah that you should have a petrol station in Chicago. Why Chicago?"

"Sidi, the brother of my wife went to America, and he has there a petrol pump in Chicago. Do I want to remain in a backward part of the world all my days? Here there is money and much food and many rugs and women—but it is not modern. It is not American."

Peters looked thoughtfully into the dignified black face. Mohammed in his white robes was a magnificent sight. What strange desires rose in the human heart!

"I don't know that you're wise," he said with a sigh, "but so be it. Of course, if we are found out—"

A smile on the black face revealed beautiful white teeth.

"Then it is death—for me certainly. Perhaps not for you, Sidi, since you are valuable."

"They deal out death rather easily here, do they?"

The shoulders of the other man rose and fell contemptuously.

"What is death? That, too, is the will of Allah."

"You know what you have to do?"

"I know, Sidi. I am to take you to the roof after dark. Also I am to put in your room clothing such as I and the other servants wear. Later—there will be other things."

"Right. You'd better let me out of the lift now. Somebody may notice we're riding up and down. It may give them ideas."

3

There was dancing going on. Andy Peters was dancing with Miss Jennsen. He held her close to him, and seemed to be murmuring in her ear. As they revolved slowly near where Hilary was standing he caught her eye and immediately gave her an outrageous wink.

Hilary, biting her lip to avoid a smile, averted her eyes quickly.

Her glance fell on Betterton who was standing just across the room talking to Torquil Ericsson. Hilary frowned a little as she watched them.

"Have a turn with me, Olive?" said Murchison's voice at her elbow.

"Yes, of course, Simon."

"Mind you, I'm not very hot at dancing," he warned her.

Hilary concentrated on keeping her feet where he could not possibly tread on them.

"It's exercise, that's what I say," said Murchison, panting slightly. He was an energetic dancer.

"Awfully jolly frock you've got on, Olive."

His conversation seemed always to come out of an old-fashioned novel.

"I'm glad you like it," said Hilary.

"Get it out of the Fashion Department?"

Resisting the temptation to reply: "Where else?" Hilary merely said, "Yes."

"Must say, you know," panted Murchison as he capered perseveringly round the floor, "they do you jolly well here. Said so to Bianca only the other day. Beats the Welfare State every time. No worries about money, or income tax—or repairs or upkeep. All the worrying done for you. Must be a wonderful life for a woman, I should say."

"Bianca finds it so, does she?"

"Well, she was restless for a bit, but now she's managed to get up a few committees and organise one or two things—debates, you know, and lectures. She's complaining that you don't take as much part as you might in things."

"I'm afraid I'm not that kind of person, Simon. I've never been very public spirited."

"Yes, but you girls have got to keep yourselves amused one way or another. At least I don't mean *amused* exactly—"

"Occupied?" suggested Hilary.

"Yes—I mean the modern woman wants to get her teeth into something. I quite realise that women like you and Bianca have made a definite sacrifice coming here —you're neither of you scientists, thank goodness— really, these scientific women! Absolutely the limit, most of them! I said to Bianca, 'Give Olive time, she's got to get tuned in.' It takes a little time getting used to this place. To begin with, one gets a kind of claustrophobic feeling. But it wears off—it wears off . . ."

"You mean—one can get used to anything?"

"Well, some people feel it more than others. Tom, now, seems to take it hard. Where's old Tom tonight?

Oh, yes, I see, over there with Torquil. Quite insepa-
rable, those two."

"I wish they weren't. I mean, I shouldn't have thought
they had very much in common."

"Young Torquil seems fascinated by your husband.
He follows him round everywhere."

"I've noticed it. I wondered—why?"

"Well, he's always got some outlandish theory to
get off his chest—it's beyond my power to follow him
—his English isn't too good, as you know. But Tom
listens and manages to take it all in."

The dance ended. Andy Peters came up and claimed
Hilary for the next one.

"I observed you suffering in a good cause," he said.
"How badly did you get trampled?"

"Oh, I was fairly agile."

"You noticed me doing my stuff?"

"With the Jennsen?"

"Yes. I think I may say without undue modesty that
I have made a hit, a palpable hit in that quarter. These
plain angular short-sighted girls respond immediately
when given the treatment."

"You certainly gave the impression of having fallen
for her."

"That was the idea. That girl, Olive, properly handled,
can be very useful. She's in the know about all the
arrangements here. For instance, tomorrow there's a
party of various V.I.P.'s due here. Doctors and a few
Government officials and a rich patron or two."

"Andy—do you think there might be a chance . . ."

"No, I don't. I bet *that's* going to be taken care of.
So don't cherish false hopes. But it will be valuable because we'll get an idea of the procedure. And on the
next occasion—well, there might be something doing.
So long as I can keep the Jennsen eating out of my

hand, I can get a lot of miscellaneous information out of her."

"How much do the people who are coming know?"

"About *us*—the Unit, I mean—nothing at all. Or so I gather. They just inspect the settlement and the medical research laboratories. This place has been deliberately built like a labyrinth, just so that nobody coming into it can possibly guess its extent. I gather there are kinds of bulkheads that close, and that shut off our area."

"It all seems so incredible."

"I know. Half the time one feels one must be dreaming. One of the unreal things here is never seeing any children about. Thank goodness there aren't! You must be thankful you haven't got a child."

He felt the sudden stiffening of her body.

"Here—I'm sorry—I said the wrong thing!" He led her off the dance floor and to a couple of chairs.

"I'm very sorry," he repeated. "I hurt you, didn't I?"

"It's nothing—no, really not your fault. I did have a child—and it died—that's all."

"You had a child?—" he stared, surprised. "I thought you'd only been married to Betterton six months?"

Olive flushed. She said quickly,

"Yes, of course. But I was—married before. I divorced my first husband."

"Oh, I see. That's the worst of this place. One doesn't know anything about people's lives before they came here, and so one goes and says the wrong thing. It's odd to realise sometimes that I don't know anything about you at all."

"Or I anything about you. How you were brought up—and where—your family—"

"I was brought up in a strictly scientific atmosphere. Nourished on test tubes, you might say. Nobody ever thought or talked of anything else. But I was never the bright boy of the family. Genius lay elsewhere."

"Where exactly?"

"A girl. She was brilliant. She might have been another Madame Curie. She could have opened up new horizons . . ."

"She—what happened to her?"

He said shortly:

"She was killed."

Hilary guessed at some wartime tragedy. She said gently,

"You cared for her?"

"More than I have ever cared for anybody."

He roused himself suddenly.

"What the heck—we've got enough troubles in the present, right here and now. Look at our Norwegian friend. Apart from his eyes, he always looks as though he were made from wood. And that wonderful little stiff bow of his—as though you'd pulled a string."

"It's because he's so very tall and thin."

"Not so very tall. About my height—five foot eleven or six foot, not more."

"Height is deceptive."

"Yes, it's like descriptions on passports. Take Ericsson. Height six foot, fair hair, blue eyes, face long, demeanour wooden, nose medium, mouth ordinary. Even add what a passport wouldn't—speaks correctly but pedantically—you still wouldn't have the first idea what Torquil really looked like. What's the matter?"

"Nothing."

She was staring across the room at Ericsson. That description of Boris Glydr! Almost word for word as she had heard it from Jessop. Was *that* why she had always felt nervous of Torquil Ericsson? Could it possibly be that— Turning abruptly to Peters she said,

"I suppose he *is* Ericsson? He couldn't be someone else?"

Peters looked at her in astonishment.

"Someone else? Who?"

"I mean—at least I think I mean—could he have come here pretending to be Ericsson?"

Peters considered.

"I suppose—no, I don't think that would be feasible. He'd have to be a scientist . . . and anyway, Ericsson is quite well known."

"But nobody here seems ever to have met him before —or I suppose he could be Ericsson, but be someone else as well."

"You mean Ericsson could have been leading some kind of double life? That's possible, I suppose. But it's not very likely."

"No," said Hilary. "No, of course it isn't likely."

Of course Ericsson was not Boris Glydr. But why should Olive Betterton have been so insistent on warning Tom against Boris? Could it have been because she knew that Boris was on his way to the Unit? Supposing the man who had come to London calling himself Boris Glydr was not Boris Glydr at all? Supposing that he was really Torquil Ericsson. The description fitted. Ever since he arrived at the Unit, he had focussed his attention on Tom. Ericsson, she was sure, was a dangerous person,—you didn't know what went on behind those pale dreamy eyes . . .

She shivered.

"Olive—what's the matter? What is it?"

"Nothing. Look. The Deputy Director is going to make an announcement."

Dr. Nielson was holding up his hand for silence. He spoke into the microphone on the platform of the Hall.

"Friends and colleagues. Tomorrow you are asked to remain in the Emergency Wing. Please assemble at

11:00 A.M. when there will be roll call. Emergency orders are for twenty-four hours only. I much regret the inconvenience. A notice has been posted on the board."

He retired smiling. The music began again.

"I must pursue the Jennsen again," said Peters. "I see her looking earnest by a pillar. I want to hear just what these Emergency quarters consist of."

He moved away. Hilary sat thinking. Was she an imaginative fool? Torquil Ericsson? Boris Glydr?

4

Roll call was in the big lecture room. Everyone was present and answered to his or her name. Then they were marshalled into a long column and marched off.

The route was, as usual, through a maze of winding corridors. Hilary, walking by Peters, knew that he had concealed in his hand, a tiny compass. From this, unobtrusively, he was calculating their direction.

"Not that it helps," he observed ruefully in a low tone. "Or at any rate it doesn't help at the moment. But it may do—some time."

At the end of the corridor they were following was a door and there was a momentary halt as the door was opened.

Peters took out his cigarette case—but immediately Van Heidem's voice was raised peremptorily.

"No smoking, please. That has already been told you."

"Sorry, sir."

Peters paused with the cigarette case in his hand. Then they all went forward again.

"Just like sheep," said Hilary disgustedly.

"Cheer up," Peters murmured. "Baa, baa, black sheep is among the flock, thinking up devilry hard."

She flashed him a grateful glance and smiled.

"Women's dormitory to the right," said Miss Jennsen. She shepherded the women off in the direction indicated.

The men were fallen off to the left.

The dormitory was a large room of hygienic appearance rather like a hospital ward. It had beds along the walls with curtains of plastic material that could be pulled for privacy. There was a locker by each bed.

"You will find arrangements rather simple," said Miss Jennsen, "but not too primitive. The bathroom accommodation is through there to the right. The communal living room is through the door at the end."

The communal living room where they all met again was plainly furnished rather like an airport waiting room—there was a bar and snack counter at one side. Along the other side was a row of book shelves.

The day passed quite agreeably. There were two cinema performances shown on a small portable screen.

The lighting was of the daylight type which tended to obscure the fact that there were no windows. Towards evening a fresh set of bulbs came on—soft and discreet night lighting.

"Clever," said Peters appreciatively. "It helps to minimise the feeling of being walled up alive."

How helpless they all were, thought Hilary. Somewhere, quite near them, were a party from the outside world. And there was no means of communicating with them, of appealing for help. As usual, everything had been ruthlessly and efficiently planned.

Peters was sitting with Miss Jennsen. Hilary suggested to the Murchisons that they should play bridge. Tom Betterton refused. He said he couldn't concentrate, but Dr. Barron made a fourth.

Oddly enough, Hilary found the game enjoyable. It was half past eleven when their third rubber came to an end, with herself and Dr. Barron the winners.

"I enjoyed that," she said. She glanced at her watch. "It's quite late. I suppose the V.I.P.'s will have left now —or do they spend the night here?"

"I don't really know," said Simon Murchison. "I believe one or two of the specially keen medicos stay over. Anyway, they'll all have gone by tomorrow midday."

"And that's when we're put back in circulation?"

"Yes. About time, too. It upsets all one's routine, this sort of thing."

"But it is well arranged," said Bianca with approval.

She and Hilary got up and said goodnight to the two men.

Hilary stood back a little to allow Bianca to precede her into the dimly lit dormitory. As she did so, she felt a soft touch on her arm.

She turned sharply to find one of the tall dark faced servants standing beside her.

He spoke in a low urgent voice in French.

"S'il vous plaît, Madame, you are to come."

"Come? Come where?"

"If you please follow me."

She stood irresolute for a moment.

Bianca had gone on into the dormitory. In the communal living room the few persons left were engaged in conversation with each other.

Again she felt that soft urgent touch on her arm.

"You will follow me please, Madame."

He moved a few steps and stood, looking back, beckoning to her. A little doubtfully Hilary followed him.

She noticed that this particular man was far more richly dressed than most of the native servants. His robes were embroidered heavily with gold thread.

He led her through a small door in a corner of the

communal living room, then once more along the inevitable anonymous white corridors. She did not think it was the same way by which they had come to the Emergency Wing, but it was always difficult to be sure because of the similarity of the passages. Once she turned to ask a question but the guide shook his head impatiently and hurried on.

He stopped finally at the end of a corridor and pressed a button in the wall. A panel slid back disclosing a small lift. He gestured her in, followed her, and the lift shot upwards.

Hilary said sharply:

"Where are you taking me?"

The dark eyes held hers in a kind of dignified reproof.

"To the Master, Madame. It is for you a great honour."

"To the Director, you mean?"

"To the Master . . ."

The lift stopped. He slid back the doors and motioned her out. Then they walked down another corridor and arrived at a door. Her guide rapped on the door and it was opened from inside. Here again were white robes, gold embroidery and a black, impassive face.

The man took Hilary across the small red-carpeted anteroom and drew aside some hangings at the further side. Hilary passed through. She found herself, unexpectedly, in an almost oriental interior. There were low couches, coffee tables, one or two beautiful rugs hanging on the walls. Sitting on a low divan was a figure at whom she stared with complete incredulity. Small, yellow, wrinkled, old, she stared unbelievingly into the smiling eyes of Mr. Aristides.

18

"Asseyez vous, chère Madame," said Mr. Aristides.

He waved a small clawlike hand, and Hilary came forward in a dream and sat down upon another low divan opposite him. He gave a gentle little cackle of laughter.

"You are surprised," he said. "It is not what you expected, eh?"

"No, indeed," said Hilary. "I never thought—I never imagined—"

But already her surprise was subsiding.

With her recognition of Mr. Aristides, the dream world of unreality in which she had been living for the past week shattered and broke. She knew now that the Unit had seemed unreal to her—because it *was* unreal. It had never been what it pretended to be. The Herr Director with his spellbinder's voice had been unreal too—a mere figurehead of fiction set up to obscure the truth. The truth was here in this secret oriental room. A little old man sitting there and laughing, quietly. With Mr. Aristides in the centre of the picture, everything made sense—hard, practical everyday sense.

"I see now," said Hilary. "This—is all yours isn't it?"

"Yes, Madame."

"And the Director? The so-called Director?"

"He is very good," said Mr. Aristides appreciatively. "I pay him a very high salary. He used to run Revivalist meetings."

He smoked thoughtfully for a moment or two. Hilary did not speak.

"There is Turkish Delight beside you, Madame. And other sweetmeats if you prefer them." Again there was a silence. Then he went on, "I am a philanthropist, Madame. As you know, I am rich. One of the richest men—possibly the richest man in the world today. With my wealth I feel under the obligation to serve humanity. I have established here, in this remote spot, a colony of lepers and a vast assembly of research into the problem of the cure of leprosy. Certain types of leprosy are curable. Others, so far, have proved incurable. But all the time we are working and obtaining good results. Leprosy is not really such an easily communicated disease. It is not half so infectious or so contagious as smallpox or typhus or plague or any of these other things. And yet, if you say to people, 'a leper colony,' they will shudder and give it a wide berth. It is an old, old fear that. A fear that you can find in the Bible, and which has existed all down through the years. The horror of the leper. It has been useful to me in establishing this place."

"You established it for that reason?"

"Yes. We have here also a Cancer Research department, and important work is being done on tuberculosis. There is virus research, also—for curative reasons, *bien entendu*—biological warfare is not mentioned. All humane, all acceptable, all redounding greatly to my honour. Well-known physicians, surgeons and research chemists come here to see our results from time to time as they have come today. The building has been cunningly constructed in such a way that a part of it is shut off and unapparent even from the air. The more secret laboratories have been tunnelled right into the rock. In any case, I am above suspicion." He smiled and added simply: "I am so very rich, you see."

"But why?" demanded Hilary. "Why this urge for destruction?"

"I have no urge for destruction, Madame. You wrong me."

"But then—I simply don't understand."

"I am a business man," said Mr. Aristides simply. "I am also a collector. When wealth becomes oppressive, that is the only thing to do. I have collected many things in my time. Pictures—I have the finest art collection in Europe. Certain kinds of ceramics. Philately —my stamp collection is famous. When a collection is fully representative, one goes on to the next thing. I am an old man, Madame, and there was not very much more for me to collect. So I came at last to collecting brains."

"Brains?" Hilary queried.

He nodded gently.

"Yes, it is the most interesting thing to collect of all. Little by little, Madame, I am assembling here all the brains of the world. The young men, those are the ones I am bringing here. Young men of promise, young men of achievement. One day the tired nations of the world will wake up and realise that their scientists are old and stale, and that the young brains of the world—the doctors, the research chemists, the physicists, the surgeons, are all here in my keeping. And if they want a scientist, or a plastic surgeon, or a biologist, they will have to come and buy him from me!"

"You mean . . ." Hilary leaned forward, staring at him. "You mean that this is all a gigantic financial operation?"

Again Mr. Aristides nodded gently.

"Yes," he said. "Naturally. Otherwise—it would not make sense, would it?"

Hilary gave a deep sigh.

"No," she said. "That's just what I've felt."

"After all, you see," said Mr. Aristides almost apologetically, "it is my profession. I am a financier."

"And you mean there is no political side to this at all? You don't want World Power—?"

He threw up his hand in rebuke.

"I do not want to be God," he said. "I am a religious man. That is the occupational disease of Dictators: wanting to be God. So far I have not contracted that disease." He reflected a moment and said: "It may come. Yes, it may come . . . But as yet, mercifully— no."

"But how do you get all these people to come here?"

"I buy them, Madame. In the open market. Like any other merchandise. Sometimes I buy them with money. More often, I buy them with ideas. Young men are dreamers. They have ideals. They have beliefs. Sometimes I buy them with safety—those that have transgressed the law."

"That explains it," said Hilary. "Explains, I mean, what puzzled me so on the journey here."

"Ah! It puzzled you on the journey, did it?"

"Yes. The difference in aims. Andy Peters, the American, seemed completely Left Wing. But Ericsson was a fanatical believer in the Superman. And Helga Needheim was a Fascist of the most arrogant and Pagan kind. Dr. Barron—" she hesitated.

"Yes, he came for money," said Aristides. "Dr. Barron is civilised and cynical. He had no illusions, but he has a genuine love of his work. He wanted unlimited money, so as to pursue his researches further." He added: "You are intelligent, Madame. I saw that at once in Fez."

He gave a gentle little cackle of laughter.

"You did not know it, Madame, but I went to Fez

simply to observe you—or rather I had you brought to Fez in order that I might observe you."

"I see," said Hilary.

She noted the oriental rephrasing of the sentence.

"I was pleased to think that you would be coming here. For, if you understand me, I do not find many intelligent people in this place to talk to." He made a gesture. "These scientists, these biologists, these research chemists, they are not interesting. They are geniuses perhaps at what they do, but they are uninteresting people with whom to converse.

"Their wives," he added thoughtfully, "are usually very dull, too. We do not encourage wives here. I permit wives to come for only one reason."

"What reason?"

Mr. Aristides said drily,

"In the rare cases where a husband is unable to do his work properly because he is thinking too much of his wife. That seemed to be the case with your husband, Thomas Betterton. Thomas Betterton is known to the world as a young man of genius, but since he has been here he has done only mediocre and second class work. Yes, Betterton has disappointed me."

"But don't you find that constantly happening? These people are, after all, in prison here. Surely they rebel? At first, at any rate?"

"Yes," Mr. Aristides agreed. "That is only natural and inevitable. It is so when you first cage a bird. But if the bird is in a big enough aviary; if it has all that it needs; a mate, seed, water, twigs, all the material of life, it forgets in the end that it was ever free."

Hilary shivered a little.

"You frighten me," she said. "You really frighten me."

"You will grow to understand many things here, Madame. Let me assure you that though all these men of different ideologies arrive here and are disillusioned and rebellious, they will all toe the line in the end."

"You can't be sure of that," said Hilary.

"One can be absolutely sure of nothing in this world. I agree with you there. But it is a ninety-five per cent certainty all the same."

Hilary looked at him with something like horror.

"It's dreadful," she said. "It's like a typists' pool! You've got a pool here of brains."

"Exactly. You put it very justly, Madame."

"And from this pool, you intend, one day, to supply scientists to whoever pays you best for them?"

"That is, roughly, the general principle, Madame."

"But you can't send out a scientist just as you can send out a typist?"

"Why not?"

"Because once your scientist is in the free world again, he could refuse to work for his new employer. He would be free again."

"True up to a point. There may have to be a certain —conditioning, shall we say?"

"Conditioning—what do you mean by that?"

"You have heard of lobotomy, Madame?"

Hilary frowned.

"That's a brain operation, isn't it?"

"But yes. It was devised originally for the curing of melancholia. I put it to you not in medical terms, Madame, but in such terms as you and I understand. After the operation the patient has no more desire to commit suicide, no further feelings of guilt. He is carefree, conscienceless and in most cases obedient."

"It hasn't been a hundred per cent success, has it?"

"In the past, no. But here we have made great strides

in the investigation of the subject. I have here three surgeons; one Russian, one Frenchman and an Austrian. By various operations of grafting and delicate manipulation of the brain, they are arriving gradually at a state where docility can be assured and the will can be controlled without necessarily affecting mental brilliance. It seems possible that we may in the end so condition a human being that while his powers of intellect remain unimpaired, he will exhibit perfect docility. Any suggestion made to him he will accept."

"But that's horrible," cried Hilary. "Horrible!"

He corrected her serenely.

"It is useful. It is even in some ways beneficent. For the patient will be happy, contented, without fears or longings or unrest."

"I don't believe it will ever happen," said Hilary defiantly.

"*Chère, Madame,* forgive me if I say you are hardly competent to speak on the subject."

"What I mean is," said Hilary, "that I do not believe a contented, suggestible animal will ever produce creative work of real brilliance."

Aristides shrugged his shoulders.

"Perhaps. You are intelligent. You may have something there. Time will show. Experiments are going on all the time."

"Experiments! On human beings, do you mean?"

"But certainly. That is the only practical method."

"But—what human beings?"

"There are always the misfits," said Aristides. "The ones who do not adapt themselves to life here, who will not cooperate. They make good experimental material."

Hilary dug her fingers into the cushions of the divan. She felt a deep horror of this smiling, yellow-faced little man with his inhuman outlook. Everything he said was so reasonable, so logical and so businesslike, that it made the horror worse. Here was no raving madman, just a man to whom his fellow creatures were so much raw material.

"Don't you believe in God?" she said.

"Naturally I believe in God." Mr. Aristides raised his eyebrows. His tone almost shocked. "I have told you already. I am a religious man. God has blessed me with supreme power. With money and opportunity."

"Do you read your Bible?" asked Hilary.

"Certainly, Madame."

"Do you remember what Moses and Aaron said to Pharaoh? *'Let my people go.'* "

He smiled.

"So—I am Pharaoh?— And you are Moses and Aaron in one? Is that what you are saying to me, Madame? To let these people go, all of them, or just— one special case?"

"I'd like to say—all of them," said Hilary.

"But you are well aware, *chère, Madame,*" he said, "that that would be a waste of time. So instead, is it not your husband for whom you plead?"

"He is no good to you," said Hilary. "Surely by now you must realise that."

"Perhaps, it is true what you say, Madame. Yes, I am very much disappointed in Thomas Betterton. I hoped that your presence here might restore him to his brilliance, for undoubtedly he has brilliance. His reputation in America leaves no doubt as to that. But your coming seems to have had little or no effect. I speak not of my own knowledge, of course, but from the reports of those fitted to know. His brother scientists who have been working with him." He shrugged his shoulders. "He does conscientious, mediocre work. No more."

"There are birds that cannot sing in captivity," said Hilary. "Perhaps there are scientists who cannot attain creative thought under certain circumstances. You must admit that that is a reasonable possibility."

"It may be so. I do not deny it."

"Then write off Thomas Betterton as one of your failures. Let him return to the outer world."

"That would hardly do, Madame. I am not yet prepared to have knowledge of this place broadcast to the globe."

"You could swear him to secrecy. He would swear never to breathe a word."

"He would swear—yes. But he would not keep that word."

"He would! Oh, indeed, he would!"

"There speaks a wife! One cannot take the word of wives on this point. Of course," he leaned back in his chair, and brought the tips of his yellow fingers together, "of course, he might leave a hostage behind him, and that might tie his tongue."

"You mean?"

"I mean you, Madame. . . . If Thomas Betterton went, and you remained as a hostage, how would that bargain strike you? Would you be willing?"

Hilary stared past him into the shadows. Mr. Aristides could not know the pictures that rose before her eyes. She was back in a hospital room, sitting by a dying woman. She was listening to Jessop and memorising his instructions. If there was a chance, now, that Thomas Betterton might go free, whilst she remained, would not that be the best way to fulfil her mission? For she knew (what Mr. Aristides did not), that there would be no hostage in the usual meaning of the word, left behind. She herself meant nothing to Thomas Betterton. The wife he had loved was already dead.

She raised her head and looked across at the little old man on the divan.

"I should be willing," she said.

"You have courage, Madame, and loyalty and devotion. They are good qualities. For the rest—" He smiled. "We will talk of it again some other time."

"Oh no, no!" Hilary suddenly buried her face in her hands. Her shoulders shook. "I can't bear it! I can't bear it! It's all too inhuman."

"You must not mind so much, Madame." The old man's voice was tender, almost soothing. "It has pleased me tonight to tell you my aims and my aspirations. It has been interesting to me to see the effect upon a mind totally unprepared. A mind like yours, well balanced, sane and intelligent. You are horrified. You are repulsed. Yet I think that to shock you in this way is a wise plan. At first you repel the idea, then you think of it, you reflect on it, and in the end it will seem to you natural; as though it has always existed, a commonplace."

"Never that!" cried Hilary. "Never that! Never! Never!"

"Ah," said Mr. Aristides. "There speaks the passion and the rebellion that go with red hair. My second wife," he added reflectively, "had red hair. She was a beautiful woman, and she loved me. Strange, is it not? I have always admired red-haired women. Your hair is very beautiful. There are other things I like about you. Your spirit, your courage; the fact that you have a mind of your own." He sighed. "Alas! Women as women interest me very little nowadays. I have a couple of young girls here who please me sometimes, but it is the stimulus of mental companionship that I now prefer. Believe me, Madame, your company has refreshed me greatly."

"Supposing I repeat all that you have told me to—my husband?"

Aristides smiled indulgently.

"Ah yes, supposing you do? But will you?"

"I don't know. I—oh, I don't know."

"Ah!" said Mr. Aristides. "You are wise. There is some knowledge women should keep to themselves. But you are tired—and upset. From time to time, when I pay my visits here, you shall be brought to me, and we will discuss many things."

"Let me leave this place—" Hilary stretched her hands out to him. "Oh let me go away. Let me leave with you when you go. Please! Please!"

He shook his head gently. His expression was indulgent, but there was a faint touch of contempt behind it.

"Now you are talking like a child," he said reprovingly. "How could I let you go? How could I let you spread the story round the world of what you have seen here?"

"Wouldn't you believe me if I swore I wouldn't say a word to anyone?"

"No indeed, I should not believe you," said Mr. Aristides. "I should be very foolish if I believed anything of the kind."

"I don't want to be here. I don't want to stay here in this prison. I want to get out."

"But you have your husband. You came here to join him, deliberately, of your own free will."

"But I didn't know what I was coming to. I'd no idea."

"No," said Aristides, "you had no idea. But I can assure you this particular world you have come to is a much pleasanter world than the life beyond the Iron Curtain. Here you have everything you need! Luxury, a beautiful climate, distractions . . ."

He got up and patted her gently on the shoulder.

"You will settle down," he said, confidently. "Ah yes,

the red-headed bird in the cage will settle down. In a year, in two years certainly, you will be very happy! Though possibly," he added thoughtfully, "less interesting."

19

HILARY AWOKE the following night with a start. She raised herself on her elbow, listening.

"Tom, do you hear?"

"Yes. Aircraft—flying low. Nothing in that. They come over from time to time."

"I wondered——" She did not finish her sentence.

She lay awake thinking, going over and over that strange interview with Aristides.

The old man had got some kind of capricious liking for her.

Could she play upon that?

Could she in the end prevail upon him to take her with him, out into the world again?

Next time he came, if he sent for her, she would lead him on to talk of his dead red-haired wife. It was not the lure of the flesh that would captivate him. His blood ran too coldly now in his veins for that. Besides he had his "young girls." But the old like to remember, to be urged on to talk of times gone by . . .

Uncle George, who had lived in Cheltenham . . .

Hilary smiled in the darkness, remembering Uncle George.

Were Uncle George and Aristides, the man of millions, really very different under the skin? Uncle George had had a housekeeper—"such a nice safe woman, my dear, not flashy or sexy or anything like that. Nice and plain and safe." But Uncle George had upset his family by marrying that nice plain woman. She had been a very good listener . . .

What had Hilary said to Tom? "I'll find a way of getting out of here"? Odd, if the way should prove to be Aristides . . .

2

"A message," said Leblanc. "A message at last."

His orderly had just entered and, after saluting, had laid a folded paper before him. He unfolded it, then spoke excitedly.

"This is a report from one of our reconnaissance pilots. He has been operating over one of the selected squares of territory. When flying over a certain position in a mountainous region he observed a signal being flashed. It was in Morse and was twice repeated. Here it is."

He laid the enclosure before Jessop.

C.O.G.L.E.P.R.O.S.I.E.S.L.

He separated off the last two letters with a pencil.

"SL—that is our code for 'Do not acknowledge.' "

"And COG with which the message starts," said Jessop, "is our recognition signal."

"Then the rest is the actual message." He underlined it. "LEPROSIE." He surveyed it dubiously.

"Leprosy?" said Jessop.

"And what does that mean?"

"Have you any important Leper Settlements? Or unimportant ones for that matter?"

Leblanc spread out a large map in front of him. He pointed with a stubby forefinger stained with nicotine.

"Here," he marked it off, "is the area over which our pilot was operating. Let me see now. I seem to recall . . ."

He left the room. Presently he returned.

"I have it," he said. "There is a very famous medical Research station, founded and endowed by well known philanthropists and operating in that area—a very deserted one, by the way. Valuable work has been done there in the study of Leprosy. There is a Leper Settlement there of about two hundred people. There is also a Cancer Research station, and a Tubercular Sanatorium. But understand this, it is all of the highest authenticity. Its reputation is of the highest. The President of the Republic himself is its Patron."

"Yes," said Jessop appreciatively. "Very nice work, in fact."

"But it is open to inspection at any time. Medical men who are interested in these subjects visit there."

"And see nothing they ought not to see! Why should they? There is no better camouflage for dubious business, than an atmosphere of the highest respectability."

"It could be," Leblanc said dubiously, "I suppose, a halting place, for parties of people bound on a journey. One or two of the mid-European doctors, perhaps, have managed to arrange something like that. A small party of people, like the one we are tracking, could lie *perdu* there for a few weeks before continuing their journey."

"I think it might be something more than that," said Jessop. "I think it might be—Journey's End."

"You think it is something—big?"

"A Leper Settlement seems to me very suggestive . . . I believe, under modern treatment, leprosy nowadays is treated at home."

"In civilised communities, perhaps. But one could not do that in this country."

"No. But the word Leprosy still has its association with the Middle Ages when the Leper carried his bell to warn away people from his path. Idle curiosity does not bring people to a Leper Settlement; the people who come are, as you say, the medical profession, interested only in the medical research done there, and possibly the social worker, anxious to report on the conditions under which the Lepers live—all of which are no doubt admirable. Behind that façade of philanthropy and charity—anything might go on. Who, by the way, owns the place? Who are the philanthropists who endowed it and set it up?"

"That is easily ascertained. A little minute."

He turned shortly, an official reference book in his hand.

"It was established by private enterprise. By a group of philanthropists of whom the chief is Aristides. As you know, he is a man of fabulous wealth, and gives generously to charitable enterprises. He has founded hospitals in Paris and also in Seville. This is, to all intents and purposes, his show—the other benefactors are a group of his associates."

"So—it's an Aristides enterprise. And Aristides was in Fez when Olive Betterton was there."

"Aristides!" Leblanc savoured the full implication. "*Mais—c'est colossal!*"

"Yes."

"*C'est fantastique!*"

"Quite."

"*Enfin—c'est formidable!*"

"Definitely."

"But do you realise how formidable it is?" Leblanc shook an excited forefinger in the other's face. "This Aristides, he has a finger in every pie. He is behind nearly everything. The banks, the Government, the manufacturing industries, armaments, transport! One never sees him, one hardly hears of him! He sits in a warm room in his Spanish castle, smoking, and sometimes he scrawls a few words on a little piece of paper and throws it on the ground, and a secretary crawls forward and picks it up, and a few days later an important banker in Paris blows his brains out! It is like that!"

"How wonderfully dramatic you are, Leblanc. But it is really not very surprising. Presidents and Ministers make important pronouncements, bankers sit back behind their sumptuous desks and roll out opulent statements—but one is never surprised to find out that behind the importance and magnificence there is somewhere some scrubby little man who is the real motive power. It is really not at all surprising to find that Aristides is behind all this disappearing business—in fact if we'd had any sense we'd have thought of it before. The whole thing's a vast commercial ramp. It's not political at all. The question is," he added, "What are we going to do about it?"

Leblanc's face grew gloomy.

"It is not going to be easy, you understand. If we are wrong—I dare not think of it! And even if we are right —we have got to prove we are right. If we make investigations—those investigations can be called off—at the highest level, you understand? No, it is not going to be easy. . . . But," he wagged an emphatic stubby forefinger, "it will be done."

20

THE CARS SWEPT UP the mountain road and stopped in front of the great gate set in the rock. There were four cars. In the first car was a French Minister and the American Ambassador, in the second car was the British Consul, a Member of Parliament and the Chief of Police. In the third car were two members of a former Royal Commission and two distinguished journalists. The complement of these three cars was made up with the necessary satellites. The fourth car contained certain people not known to the general public, but sufficiently distinguished in their own sphere. They included Captain Leblanc and Mr. Jessop. The chauffeurs, immaculately garbed, were now opening car doors and bowing as they assisted the distinguished visitors to alight.

"One hopes," murmured the Minister, apprehensively, "that there will be no possibility of a contact of any kind."

One of the satellites immediately made soothing noises.

"*Du tout, M. le Ministre.* Every suitable precaution is taken. One inspects only from a distance."

The Minister, who was elderly and apprehensive, looked relieved. The Ambassador said something about the better understanding and treatment of these diseases nowadays.

The great gates were flung open. On the threshold stood a small party bowing to welcome them. The Director, dark, thickset, the Deputy Director, big and fair, two distinguished doctors and a distinguished Research Chemist. The greetings were French, florid and prolonged.

"And *ce cher* Aristides," demanded the Minister. "I sincerely hope ill health has not prevented him from fulfilling his promise to meet us here."

"M. Aristides flew from Spain yesterday," said the Deputy Director. "He awaits you within. Permit me, Your Excellency—M. le Ministre, to lead the way."

The party followed him. M. le Ministre, who was slightly apprehensive, glanced through the heavy railings to his right. The lepers were drawn up to attention in a serried row as far as possible from the grating. The Minister looked relieved. His feelings about leprosy were still mediaeval.

In the well furnished modern lounge Mr. Aristides was awaiting his guests. There were bows, compliments, introductions. Aperitifs were served by the dark-faced servants dressed in their white robes and turbans.

"It's a wonderful place you have here, sir," said one of the younger journalists to Aristides.

The latter made one of his Oriental gestures.

"I am proud of this place," he said. "It is, as you might say, my swan song. My final gift to humanity. No expense has been spared."

"I'll say that's so," said one of the doctors on the staff, heartily. "This place is a professional man's dream. We do pretty well in the States, but what I've seen since I came here . . . and we're getting results! Yes, sir, we certainly are getting results."

His enthusiasm was of a contagious kind.

"We must make all acknowledgements to private enterprise," said the Ambassador, bowing politely to Mr. Aristides.

Mr. Aristides spoke with humility.

"God has been very good to me," he said.

Sitting hunched up in his chair he looked like a small yellow toad. The Member of Parliament murmured to the member of the Royal Commission who was very old and deaf, that he presented a very interesting paradox.

"That old rascal has probably ruined millions of people," he murmured, "and having made so much money, he doesn't know what to do with it, so he pays it back with the other hand."

The elderly judge to whom he spoke, murmured,

"One wonders to what extent results justify increased expenditure. Most of the great discoveries that have benefited the human race have been discovered with quite simple equipment."

"And now," said Aristides, when the civilities were accomplished and the aperitifs drunk, "you will honour me by partaking of a simple repast which awaits you. Dr. Van Heidem will act as your host. I myself am on a diet and eat very little these days. After the repast you will start on your tour of our building."

Under the leadership of the genial Dr. Van Heidem, the guests moved enthusiastically into the dining room. They had had two hours' flight followed by an hour's drive by car and they were all sharp set. The food was delicious and was commented on with special approval by the Minister.

"We enjoy our modest comforts," said Van Heidem. "Fresh fruit and vegetables are flown to us twice a week, arrangements are made for meat and chicken and we have, of course, substantial deep freezing units. The body must claim its due from the resources of science."

The meal was accompanied by choice vintages. After it Turkish coffee was served. The party was then asked to start on its tour of inspection. The tour took two hours and was most comprehensive. The Minister, for one, was glad when it finished. He was quite dazed by the gleaming laboratories, the endless white, shining corridors, and still more dazed by the mass of scientific detail handed out to him.

Though the Minister's interest was perfunctory, some of the others were more searching in their enquiries. Some curiosity was displayed as to the living conditions of the personnel and various other details. Dr. Van Heidem showed himself only too willing to shcw the guests all there was to see. Leblanc and Jessop, the former in attendance on the Minister and the latter accompanying the British Consul, fell a little behind the others as they all retired to the lounge.

"There is no trace here, nothing," murmured Leblanc in an agitated manner.

"Not a sign."

"Mon cher, if we have, as your saying is, barked up the wrong tree, what a catastrophe. After the weeks it has taken to arrange all this! As for me—it will finish my career."

"We're not licked yet," said Jessop. "Our friends are here, I'm sure of it."

"There is no trace of them."

"Of course there is no trace. They could not afford to have a trace of them. For these official visits everything is prepared and arranged."

"Then how are we to get our evidence? I tell you, without evidence no one will move in the matter. They are sceptical, all of them. The Minister, the American Ambassador, the British Consul—they say all of them, that a man like Aristides is above suspicion."

"Keep calm, Leblanc, keep calm. I tell you we're not licked yet."

Leblanc shrugged his shoulders.

"You have the optimism, my friend," he said. He

turned for a moment to speak to one of the immaculately arrayed moon-faced young men who formed part of the *entourage,* then turned back to Jessop and asked suspiciously: "Why are you smiling?"

"Heard of a Geiger counter?"

"Naturally. But I am not a scientist, you understand."

"No more am I. It is a very sensitive detector of radio-activity."

"And so?"

"Our friends are here. The Geiger counter tells me that. It imparts a message to say that our friends are here. This building has been purposely built in a confusing manner. All the corridors and the rooms so resemble each other that it is difficult to know where one is or what the plan of the building can be. There is a part of this place that we have not seen. It has not been shown to us."

"But you deduce that it is there because of some radio-active indication?"

"Exactly."

"In fact, it is the pearls of Madame all over again?"

"Yes. We're still playing Hansel and Gretel, as you might say. But the signs left here cannot be so apparent or so crude as the bead of a pearl necklace, or a hand of phosphoric paint. They cannot be seen, but they can be sensed . . . by our radio-active detector—"

"But, *mon Dieu,* Jessop, is that enough?"

"It should be," said Jessop. "What one is afraid of . . ." He broke off.

Leblanc finished the sentence for him.

"What you mean is that these people will not want to believe. They have been unwilling from the start. Oh yes, that is so. Even your British Consul is a man of caution. Your government at home is indebted to

Aristides in many ways. As for our government," he shrugged his shoulders. "M. le Ministre, I know, will be exceedingly hard to convince."

"We won't put our faith in governments," said Jessop. "Governments and diplomats have their hands tied. But we've got to have them here, because they're the only ones with authority. But as far as believing is concerned, I'm pinning my faith elsewhere."

"And on what in particular do you pin your faith, my friend?"

Jessop's solemn face suddenly relaxed into a grin.

"There's the press," he said. "Journalists have a nose for news. They don't want it hushed up. They're ready always to believe anything that remotely can be believed. The other person I have faith in," he went on, "is that very deaf old man."

"Aha, I know the one you mean. The one who looks as though he crumbles to his grave."

"Yes, he's deaf and infirm and semi-blind. But he's interested in truth. He's a former Lord Chief Justice, and though he may be deaf and blind and shaky on his legs, his mind's as keen as ever—he's got that keen sense that legal luminaries acquire—of knowing when there's something fishy about and someone's trying to prevent it being brought into the open. He's a man who'll listen, and will want to listen, to evidence."

They had arrived back now in the lounge. Both tea and aperitifs were provided. The Minister congratulated Mr. Aristides in well-rounded periods. The American Ambassador added his quota. It was then that the Minister, looking round him, said in a slightly nervous tone of voice,

"And now, gentlemen, I think the time has come for us to leave our kind host. We have seen all there is to see . . ." his tone dwelt on those last words with some significance, "all here is magnificent. An establishment of the first class! We are most grateful for the hospitality of our kind host, and we congratulate him on the achievement here. So we say our farewells now and depart. I am right, am I not?"

The words were, in a sense, conventional enough. The manner, too, was conventional. The glance that swept round the assembly of guests might have been no more than courtesy. Yet in actuality the words were a plea. In effect, the Minister was saying, "You've seen, gentlemen, there is nothing here, nothing of what you suspected and feared. That is a great relief and we can now leave with a clear conscience."

But in the silence a voice spoke. It was the quiet, deferential, well-bred English voice of Mr. Jessop. He spoke to the Minister in a Britannic though idiomatic French.

"With your permission, Sir," he said, "and if I may do so, I would like to ask a favour of our kind host."

"Certainly, certainly. Of course, Mr.—ah—Mr. Jessop—yes, yes?"

Jessop addressed himself solemnly to Dr. Van Heidem. He did not look ostensibly to Mr. Aristides.

"We've met so many of your people," he said. "Quite bewildering. But there's an old friend of mine here that I'd rather like to have a word with. I wonder if it could be arranged before I go?"

"A friend of yours?" Dr. Van Heidem said politely, surprised.

"Well, two friends really," said Jessop. "There's a woman, Mrs. Betterton. Olive Betterton. I believe her husband's working here. Tom Betterton. Used to be at Harwell and before that in America. I'd very much like to have a word with them both before I go."

Dr. Van Heidem's reactions were perfect. His eyes

opened in wide and polite surprise. He frowned in a puzzled way.

"Betterton—Mrs. Betterton—no, I'm afraid we have no one of that name here."

"There's an American, too," said Jessop. "Andrew Peters. Research chemistry, I believe, is his line. I'm right, sir, aren't I?" He turned deferentially to the American Ambassador.

The Ambassador was a shrewd, middle-aged man with keen blue eyes. He was a man of character as well as diplomatic ability. His eyes met Jessop's. He took a full minute to decide, and then he spoke.

"Why, yes," he said. "That's so. Andrew Peters. I'd like to see him."

Van Heidem's polite bewilderment grew. Jessop unobtrusively shot a quick glance at Aristides. The little yellow face betrayed no knowledge of anything amiss, no surprise, no disquietude. He looked merely uninterested.

"Andrew Peters? No, I'm afraid, Your Excellency, you've got your facts wrong. We've no one of that name here. I'm afraid I don't even know the name."

"You know the name of Thomas Betterton, don't you?" said Jessop.

Just for a second Van Heidem hesitated. His head turned very slightly toward the old man in the chair, but he caught himself back in time.

"Thomas Betterton," he said. "Why, yes, I think—"

One of the gentlemen of the press spoke up quickly on that cue.

"Thomas Betterton," he said. "Why, I should say he was pretty well big news. Big news six months ago when he disappeared. Why, he's made headlines in the papers all over Europe. The police have been looking for him here, there and everywhere. Do you mean to say he's been here in this place all the time?"

"No." Van Heidem spoke sharply. "Someone, I fear, has been misinforming you. A hoax, perhaps. You have seen today all our workers at the Unit. You have seen everything."

"Not quite everything I think," said Jessop, quietly. "There's a young man called Ericsson, too," he added, "and Dr. Louis Barron, and possibly Mrs. Calvin Baker."

"Ah." Dr. Van Heidem seemed to receive enlightenment. "But those people were killed in Morocco—in a plane crash. I remember it perfectly now. At least I remember Ericsson was in the crash and Dr. Louis Barron. Ah, France sustained a great loss that day. A man such as Louis Barron is hard to replace." He shook his head. "I do not know anything about a Mrs. Calvin Baker, but I do seem to remember that there was an English or American woman on that plane. It might well perhaps have been this Mrs. Betterton, of whom you speak. Yes, it was all very sad." He looked across enquiringly at Jessop. "I do not know, Monsieur, why you should suppose that these people were coming here. It may possibly be that Dr. Barron mentioned at one time that he hoped to visit our settlement here while he was in North Africa. That may possibly have given rise to a misconception."

"So you tell me," said Jessop, "that I am mistaken? That these people are none of them here."

"But how can they be, my dear sir, since they were all killed in this plane accident. The bodies were recovered, I believed."

"The bodies recovered were too badly charred for identification." Jessop spoke the last words with deliberation and significance.

There was a little stir behind him. A thin, precise, very attenuated voice said,

"Do I understand you to say that there was no precise identification?" Lord Alverstoke was leaning forward, his hand to his ear. Under bushy, overhanging eyebrows his small keen eyes looked into Jessop's.

"There could be no formal identification, my lord," said Jessop, "and I have reason to believe these people survived that accident."

"Believe?" said Lord Alverstoke, with displeasure in his thin, high voice.

"I should have said I have evidence of survival."

"Evidence? Of what nature, Mr.—er—er—Jessop."

"Mrs. Betterton was wearing a choker of false pearls on the day she left Fez for Marrakesh," said Jessop. "One of these pearls was found at a distance of half a mile from the burnt out plane."

"How can you state positively that the pearl found actually came from Mrs. Betterton's necklace?"

"Because all the pearls of that necklace had had a mark put upon them invisible to the naked eye, but recognisable under a strong lens."

"Who put that mark on them?"

"I did, Lord Alverstoke, in the presence of my colleague, here, Monsieur Leblanc."

"You put those marks—you had a reason in marking those pearls in that fashion?"

"Yes, my lord. I had reason to believe that Mrs. Betterton would lead me to her husband, Thomas Betterton, against whom a warrant is out." Jessop continued. "Two more of these pearls came to light. Each on stages of a route between where the plane was burnt out and the settlement where we now are. Enquiries in the places where these pearls were found resulted in a description of six people, roughly approximating to those people who were supposed to have been burnt in the plane. One of these passengers had also been supplied with a glove impregnated with luminous phosphorous paint. That mark was found on a car which had transported these passengers part of the way here."

Lord Alverstoke remarked in his dry, judicial voice, "Very remarkable."

In the big chair Mr. Aristides stirred. His eyelids blinked once or twice rapidly. Then he asked a question.

"Where were the last traces of this party of people found?"

"At a disused airfield, Sir." He gave precise location.

"That is many hundreds of miles from here," said Mr. Aristides. "Granted that your very interesting speculations are correct, that for some reason the accident was faked, these passengers, I gather, then took off from this disused airport for some unknown destination. Since that airport is many hundreds of miles from here, I really cannot see on what you base your belief that these people are here. Why should they be?"

"There are certain very good reasons, sir. A signal was picked up by one of our searching aeroplanes. The signal was brought to Monsieur Leblanc here. Commencing with a special code recognition signal, it gave the information that the people in question were at a Leper Settlement."

"I find this remarkable," said Mr. Aristides. "Very remarkable. But it seems to me that there is no doubt that an attempt has been made to mislead you. These people are not here." He spoke with a quiet, definite decision. "You are at perfect liberty to search the settlement if you like."

"I doubt if we should find anything, sir," said Jessop, "not, that is, by a superficial search, although," he added deliberately, "I am aware of the area at which the search should begin."

"Indeed! And where is that?"

"In the fourth corridor from the second laboratory turning to the left at the end of the passage there."

There was an abrupt movement from Dr. Van Heidem. Two glasses crashed from the tables to the floor. Jessop looked at him, smiling.

"You see, Doctor," he said, "we are well informed."

Van Heidem said sharply, "It's preposterous. Absolutely preposterous! You are suggesting that we are detaining people here against their will. I deny that categorically."

The Minister said uncomfortably,

"We seem to have arrived at an *impasse.*"

Mr. Aristides said gently,

"It has been an interesting theory. But it is only a theory." He glanced at his watch. "You will excuse me, gentlemen, if I suggest that you should leave now. You have a long drive back to the airport, and there will be alarm felt if your plane is overdue."

Both Leblanc and Jessop realised that it had come now to the showdown. Aristides was exerting all the force of his considerable personality. He was daring these men to oppose his will. If they persisted, it meant that they were willing to come out into the open against him. The Minister, as per his instructions, was anxious to capitulate. The Chief of Police was anxious only to be agreeable to the Minister. The American Ambassador was not satisfied, but he, too, would hesitate for diplomatic reasons to insist. The British Consul would have to fall in with the other two.

The journalists—Aristides considered the journalists —the journalists could be attended to! Their price might come high but he was of the opinion that they could be bought. And if they could not be bought— well, there were other ways.

As for Jessop and Leblanc, they knew. That was clear, but they could not act without authority. His eyes went on and met the eyes of a man as old as himself, cold, legal eyes. This man, he knew, could not be bought. But after all . . . His thoughts were interrupted by the sound of that cold, clear, far away little voice.

"I am of the opinion," said the voice, "that we should not unduly hurry our departure. For there is a case here that it seems to me would bear further enquiry. Grave allegations have been made and should not, I consider, be allowed to drop. In fairness every opportunity should be given to rebut them."

"The onus of proof," said Mr. Aristides, "is on you." He made a graceful gesture towards the company. "A preposterous accusation has been made, unsupported by any evidence."

"Not unsupported."

Dr. Van Heidem swung round in surprise. One of the Moroccan servants had stepped forward. He was a fine figure of a man in white embroidered robes with a white turban surrounding his head, his face gleamed black and oily.

What caused the entire company to gaze at him in speechless astonishment was the fact that from his full rather Negroid lips a voice of purely trans-Atlantic origin was proceeding.

"Not unsupported," that voice said, "you can take my evidence here and now. These gentlemen have denied that Andrew Peters, Torquil Ericsson, Mr. and Mrs. Betterton and Dr. Louis Barron are here. That's false. They're all here—and I speak for them." He took a step forward towards the American Ambassador. "You may find me a bit difficult to recognise at the moment, Sir," he said, "but I am Andrew Peters."

A very faint, sibilant hiss issued from Aristides' lips; then he settled back in his chair, his face impassive once more.

"There's a whole crowd of people hidden away here," said Peters. "There's Schwartz of Munich: there's Helga Needheim; there are Jeffreys and Davidson, the English scientists; there's Paul Wade from the U.S.A.; there are the Italians, Ricochetti and Bianco; there's Murchison. They're all right here in this building. There's a system of closing bulkheads that's quite impossible to detect by the naked eye. There's a whole network of secret laboratories cut right down into the rock."

"God bless my soul," ejaculated the American Ambassador. He looked searchingly at the dignified African figure, and then he began to laugh. "I wouldn't say I recognise you even now," he said.

"That's the injection of paraffin in the lips, sir, to say nothing of black pigment."

"If you're Peters, what's the number you go under in the F.B.I.?"

"813471, sir."

"Right," said the Ambassador, "and the initials of your other name?"

"B.A.B.D.G. sir."

The Ambassador nodded.

"This man is Peters," he said. He looked towards the Minister.

The Minister hesitated, then cleared his throat.

"You claim," he demanded of Peters, "that people are being detained here against their will?"

"Some are here willingly, Excellence, and some are not."

"In that case," said the Minister, "statements must be taken—er—yes, yes, statements must certainly be taken."

He looked at the Prefect of Police. The latter stepped forward.

"Just a moment, please." Mr. Aristides raised a

hand. "It would seem," he said, in a gentle, precise voice, "that my confidence here has been greatly abused." His cold glance went from Van Heidem to the Director and there was implacable command in it. "As to what you have permitted yourselves to do, gentlemen, in your enthusiasm for science, I am not as yet quite clear. My endowment of this place was purely in the interests of research. I have taken no part in the practical application of its policy. I would advise you, Monsieur le Directeur, if this accusation is borne out by facts, to produce immediately those people who are suspected of being detained here unlawfully."

"But, Monsieur, it is impossible. I—it will be—"

"Any experiment of that kind," said Mr. Aristides, "is at an end." His calm, financier's gaze swept over his guests. "I need hardly assure you, Messieurs," he said, "that if anything illegal is going on here, it has been no concern of mine."

It was an order, and understood as such because of his wealth, because of his power and because of his influence. Mr. Aristides, that world-famous figure, would not be implicated in this affair. Yet, even though he himself escaped unscathed, it was nevertheless defeat. Defeat for his purpose, defeat for that brains pool from which he had hoped to profit so greatly. Mr. Aristides was unperturbed by failure. It had happened to him occasionally in the course of his career. He had always accepted it philosophically and gone on to the next *coup*.

He made an oriental gesture of his hand.

"I wash my hands of this affair," he said.

The Prefect of Police bustled forward. He had had his cue now, he knew what his instructions were and he was prepared to go ahead with the full force of his official position.

"I want no obstructions," he said. "It is my duty."

His face very pale, Van Heidem stepped forward.

"If you will come this way," he said, "I will show you our reserve accommodation."

21

"OH, I FEEL AS IF I'd woken up out of a nightmare," sighed Hilary.

She stretched her arms wide above her head. They were sitting on the terrace of the hotel in Tangier. They had arrived there that morning by plane. Hilary went on,

"Did it all happen? It can't have!"

"It happened all right," said Tom Betterton, "but I agree with you, Olive, it was a nightmare. Ah well, I'm out of it now."

Jessop came along the terrace and sat down beside them.

"Where's Andy Peters?" asked Hilary.

"He'll be here presently," said Jessop. "He has a bit of business to attend to."

"So Peters was one of your people," said Hilary, "and he did things with phosphorus and a lead cigarette case that squirted radio-active material. I never knew a thing about that."

"No," said Jessop, "you were both very discreet with each other. Strictly speaking, though, he isn't one of my people. He represents the U.S.A."

"That's what you meant by saying that if I actually reached Tom here, you hoped I should have protection? You meant Andy Peters."

Jessop nodded.

"I hope you're not blaming me," said Jessop in his

most owl-like manner, "for not providing you with the desired end of your experience."

Hilary looked puzzled. "What end?"

"A more sporting form of suicide," he said.

"Oh, that!" She shook her head incredulously. "That seems just as unreal as anything else. I've been Olive Betterton so long now that I'm feeling quite confused to be Hilary Craven again."

"Ah," said Jessop, "there is my friend, Leblanc. I must go and speak to him."

He left them and walked along the terrace. Tom Betterton said, quickly,

"Do one more thing for me, will you Olive? I call you Olive still—I've got used to it."

"Yes, of course. What is it?"

"Walk along the terrace with me, then come back here and say that I've gone up to my room to lie down."

She looked at him questioningly.

"Why? What are you—"

"I'm off, my dear, while the going's good."

"Off, where?"

"Anywhere."

"But why?"

"Use your head, my dear girl. I don't know what the status is here. Tangier is an odd sort of place not under the jurisdiction of any particular country. But I know what'll happen if I come with the rest of you to Gibraltar. The first thing that'll happen when I get there, I shall be arrested."

Hilary looked at him with concern. In the excitement of their escape from the Unit, she had forgotten Tom Betterton's troubles.

"You mean the Official Secrets Act, or whatever they call it? But you can't really hope to get away can you, Tom? Where can you go?"

"I've told you. Anywhere."

"But is that feasible nowadays? There's money and all sorts of difficulties."

He gave a short laugh.

"The money's all right. It's salted away where I can get at it under a new name."

"So you did take money?"

"Of course I took money."

"But they'll track you down."

"They'll find it hard to do that. Don't you realise, Olive, that the description they'll have of me is quite unlike my present appearance. That's why I was so keen on this plastic surgery business. That's been the whole point, you see. To get away from England, bank some money, have my appearance altered in such a way that I'm safe for life."

Hilary looked at him doubtfully.

"You're wrong," she said. "I'm sure you're wrong. It'd be far better to go back and face the music. After all, it's not war time. You'd only get a short term of imprisonment, I expect. What's the good of being hounded for the rest of your life?"

"You don't understand," he said. "You don't understand the first thing about it all. Come on, let's get going. There's no time to lose."

"But how are you going to get away from Tangier?"

"I'll manage. Don't you worry."

She got up from her seat and walked with him slowly along the terrace. She felt curiously inadequate and tongue-tied. She had fulfilled her obligations to Jessop and also to the dead woman, Olive Betterton. Now there was no more to do. She and Tom Betterton had shared weeks of the closest association and yet she felt they were still strangers to each other. No bond of fellowship or friendship had grown up between them.

They reached the end of the terrace. There was a small side door there through the wall which led out on to a narrow road which curved down the hill to the port.

"I shall slip out this way," Betterton said, "nobody's watching. So long."

"Good luck to you," said Hilary slowly.

She stood there watching Betterton as he went to the door and turned its handle. As the door opened he stepped back a pace and stopped. Three men stood in the doorway. Two of them entered and came towards him. The first spoke formally.

"Thomas Betterton, I have here a warrant for your arrest. You will be held here in custody whilst extradition proceedings are taken."

Betterton turned sharply, but the other man had moved quickly round the other side of him. Instead, he turned back with a laugh.

"It's quite all right," he said, "except that I'm not Thomas Betterton."

The third man moved in through the doorway, came to stand by the side of the other two.

"Oh yes, you are," he said. "You're Thomas Betterton."

Betterton laughed.

"What you mean is that for the last month you've been living with me and hearing me called Thomas Betterton and hearing me call myself Thomas Betterton. The point is that I'm not Thomas Betterton. I met Betterton in Paris, I came on and took his place. Ask this lady if you don't believe me," he said. "She came to join me, pretending to be my wife, and I recognised her as my wife. I did, didn't I?"

Hilary nodded her head.

"That," said Betterton, "was because not being Thomas Betterton, naturally I didn't know Thomas Betterton's wife from Adam. I thought she was Thomas Betterton's wife. Afterwards I had to think up some sort of explanation that would satisfy her. But that's the truth."

"So that's why you pretended to know me," cried Hilary. "When you told me to play up—to keep up the deception!"

Betterton laughed again, confidently.

"I'm not Betterton," he said. "Look at any photograph of Betterton and you'll see I'm speaking the truth."

Peters stepped forward. His voice when he spoke was totally unlike the voice of the Peters that Hilary had known so well. It was quiet and implacable.

"I've seen photographs of Betterton," he said, "and I agree I wouldn't have recognised you as the man. But you are Thomas Betterton all the same, and I'll prove it."

He seized Betterton with a sudden strong grasp and tore off his jacket.

"If you're Thomas Betterton," he said, "you've got a scar in the shape of a Z in the crook of your right elbow."

As he spoke he ripped up the shirt and bent back Betterton's arm.

"There you are," he said, pointing triumphantly. "There are two lab assistants in the U.S.A. who'll testify to that. I know about it because Elsa wrote and told me when you did it."

"Elsa?" Betterton stared at him. He began to shake nervously. "Elsa? What about Elsa?"

"Ask what the charge is against you!"

The police official stepped forward once more.

"The charge," he said, "is murder in the first degree. Murder of your wife, Elsa Betterton."

22

"I'M SORRY, OLIVE. You've got to believe I'm sorry. About you, I mean. For your sake I'd have given him one chance. I warned you that he'd be safer to stay in the Unit and yet I'd come half way across the world to get him, and I meant to get him for what he did to Elsa."

"I don't understand. I don't understand anything. Who are you?"

"I thought you knew that. I'm Boris Andrei Pavlov Glydr, Elsa's cousin. I was sent over to America from Poland, to the University there to complete my education. And the way things were in Europe my uncle thought it best for me to take out American citizenship. I took the name of Andrew Peters. Then, when the war came, I went back to Europe. I worked for the Resistance. I got my uncle and Elsa out of Poland and they got to America. Elsa—I've told you about Elsa already. She was one of the first-class scientists of our time. It was Elsa who discovered ZE fission. Betterton was a young Canadian who was attached to Mannheim to help him in his experiments. He knew his job, but there was no more to him than that. He deliberately made love to Elsa and married her so as to be associated with her in the scientific work she was doing. When her experiments neared completion and he realised what a big thing ZE fission was going to be, he deliberately poisoned her."

"Oh, no, no."

"Yes. There were no suspicions at the time. Betterton appeared heartbroken, threw himself with renewed ardour into his work and then announced the ZE fission discovery as his own. It brought him what he wanted. Fame and the recognition of being a first-class scientist. He thought it prudent after that to leave America and come to England. He went to Harwell and worked there.

"I was tied up in Europe for some time after the war ended. Since I had a good knowledge of German, Russian and Polish, I could do very useful work there. The letter that Elsa had written to me before she died disquieted me. The illness from which she was suffering and from which she died seemed to me mysterious and unaccounted for. When at last I got back to the U.S.A. I started instituting enquiries. We won't go into it all, but I found what I was looking for. Enough, that is, to apply for an Order of Exhumation of the body. There was a young fellow in the District Attorney's office who had been a great friend of Betterton. He was going over on a trip to Europe about that time, and I think that he visited Betterton and in the course of his visit mentioned the exhumation. Betterton got the wind up. I imagine that he'd been already approached by agents of our friend, Mr. Aristides. Anyway he now saw that there lay his best chance to avoid being arrested and tried for murder. He accepted the terms, stipulating that his facial appearance was to be completely changed. What actually happened, of course, was that he found himself in a very real captivity. Moreover, he found himself in a dangerous position there since he was quite unable to deliver the goods—the scientific goods, that is to say. He was not and never had been, a man of genius."

"And you followed him?"

"Yes. When the newspapers were full of the sensational disappearance of the scientist, Thomas Betterton, I came over to England. A rather brilliant scientist friend of mine had had certain overtures made to him by a woman, a Mrs. Speeder, who worked for UNO. I discovered on arriving in England that she had had a meeting with Betterton. I played up to her, expressing Left Wing views, rather exaggerating perhaps my scientific abilities. I thought, you see, that Betterton had gone behind the Iron Curtain where no one could reach him. Well, if nobody else could reach him, I was going to reach him." His lips set in a grim line. "Elsa was a first-class scientist, and she was a beautiful and gentle woman. She'd been killed and robbed by the man whom she loved and trusted. If necessary I was going to kill Betterton with my own hands."

"I see," said Hilary, "oh, I see now."

"I wrote to you," said Peters, "when I got to England. Wrote to you, that is, in my Polish name, telling you the facts." He looked at her. "I suppose you didn't believe me. You never answered." He shrugged his shoulders. "Then I went to the Intelligence people. At first I went there putting on an act. Polish officer. Stiff, foreign and correctly formal. I was suspicious just then of everybody. However, in the end Jessop and I got together." He paused. "This morning my quest has come to an end. Extradition will be applied for, Betterton will go to the U.S.A. and will stand his trial there. If he's acquitted, I have no more to say." He added grimly, "But he won't be acquitted. The evidence is too strong."

He paused, staring down over the sunlit gardens towards the sea.

"The hell of it is," he said, "that you came out there to join him and I met you and fell in love with you. It has been hell, Olive. Believe me. So there we are. I'm the man who's responsible for sending your husband to the electric chair. We can't get away from it. It's a thing that you'll never be able to forget even if you forgave it." He got up. "Well, I wanted to tell you the whole story from my own lips. This is goodbye." He turned abruptly as Hilary stretched out a hand.

"Wait," she said, "wait. There is something you don't know. I'm not Betterton's wife. Betterton's wife, Olive Betterton, died at Casablanca. Jessop persuaded me to take her place."

He wheeled round staring at her.

"You're not Olive Betterton?"

"No."

"Good Lord," said Andy Peters. "Good Lord!" He dropped heavily into a chair beside her. "Olive," he said, "Olive, my darling."

"Don't call me Olive. My name's Hilary. Hilary Craven."

"Hilary?" He said it questioningly. "I'll have to get used to that." He put his hand over hers.

At the other end of the terrace Jessop, discussing with Leblanc various technical difficulties in the present situation, broke off in the middle of a sentence.

"You were saying?" he asked absently.

"I said, *mon cher,* that it does not seem to me that we are going to be able to proceed against this animal of an Aristides."

"No, no, Aristides always wins. That is to say he always manages to squirm out from under. But he'll have lost a lot of money, and he won't like that. And even Aristides can't keep death at bay for ever. I should say he'll be coming up before the Supreme Justice before very long, from the look of him."

"What was it attracting your attention, my friend?"

"Those two," said Jessop. "I sent Hilary Craven off

on a journey to a destination unknown, but it seems to me that her journey's end is the usual one after all."

Leblanc looked puzzled for a moment then he said, "Aha! Yes! Your Shakespeare!"

"You Frenchmen are so well read," said Jessop.